GREEN HELL

Jack Taylor has hit rock bottom: one of his best friends is dead, and the other has stopped speaking to him; he has given up battling his addiction to alcohol and other substances; and his firing from the Irish national police is by now ancient history. But Jack isn't about to embark upon a self-improvement plan. Instead, he has taken up a vigilante case against a respected professor of literature who has developed a savage habit his friends in high places are only too happy to ignore. Between pub crawls and violent outbursts, Jack's vengeful plot against the professor soon spirals toward chaos, putting both himself and his new student sidekick in danger. Ireland may be known as a "green Eden," but in Jack Taylor's world, the national color has a decidedly lethal sheen . . .

GREEN HELL
A JACK TAYLOR NOVEL

KEN BRUEN

INCLUDING A BIOGRAPHY OF JACK TAYLOR, BY BORU KENNEDY

LARGE
PRINT

First published in 2015
by
The Mysterious Press
an imprint of Grove Atlantic

First Isis Edition
published 2016
by arrangement with
the Abner Stein Agency,
via the Philip G. Spitzer Literary Agency

A catalogue record for this book is available
from the British Library.

ISBN 978–1–78541–267–7 (hb)
ISBN 978–1–78541–273–8 (nb)

Published by
F. A. Thorpe (Publishing)
Anstey, Leicestershire

Set by Words & Graphics Ltd.
Anstey, Leicestershire
Printed and bound in Great Britain by
T. J. International Ltd., Padstow, Cornwall

This book is printed on acid-free paper

For
my friends
JOHN CASSERLEY and OWEN DAGLISH
and Damanja and Prodrag Finei
(The Lights of Bosnia)

Part I

*Forgiveness
Might Be Feeding
the Hand that
Bites You*

The day began . . . badly.

For Jack, this was like breathing. Natural.

It was never a plan to write about Jack Taylor. I'd come to Dublin as part of a Rhodes scholarship to conclude a treatise on Beckett. To end up living in Galway, drinking as if I meant it,

. . . how'd that happen?

As Jack would say,

"Fuck knows."

This is not . . .

A Boswell to Dr. Johnson

Or even . . .

A Watson to Holmes gig.

But rather a haphazard series of events leading me to abandon Beckett in pursuit of the Taylor enigma. Little did I know it would be an ironic reflection of one of Jack's favorite novels:

The Wrong Case.

As Jim Crumley had once said of a book,

"This is not a crime novel, it's a story with some crimes in it."

Quite.

★   ★   ★

I met Jack Taylor at a time of odd disturbance.

James Gandolfini,

Cory Monteith,

Alan Whicker

Had all recently died. Jack mourned all three. He had heard of only the first. The second was the star of *Glee* and the third had presented a show called

Whicker's World.

Jack said those last two represented (a) the youth he never had and (b) how old he was not to recall Whicker.

Both ends of his booze-soaked candle. James G of course was in *The Sopranos*, demonstrating, Jack said,

"How depression and brutality are uneven dance partners."

This, like many things he said, made sense only to him.

I hadn't, he claimed,

"Drunk enough."

To truly grasp absurdity. Accounts in part for my name. My mother is Irish and steeped in the iconography of a blood saturated in epic/tragic history and so, after

Brian Boru

My first name.

My father hails from Boston though, alas, is not of the infamous immediate family. Though they do say all Kennedys are related.

Yeah, right!

That dog doesn't hunt. I haven't come within a spit of the Hyannis Port compound. I will admit to a certain strain of impetuousness. Spring break in Cancún the year of my graduation, I came to from a tequila slammer ruin with a tattoo on my arm, reading

P.T. 108.

When I'd jokingly suggested to Taylor I write of his life, he'd gone deep.

Then,

"Do a Tom Waits."

"Huh?"

He sighed, said,

"Shall I tell you the truth or just string you along?"

The heft of the man. Jack was, he claimed, exactly six feet tall, adding,

"Like the Pale Nazarene."

For such a ferocious derider of the Church, he was sodden with its

ritual,   innuendo,

propaganda.

I'd told him I was an atheist and he laughed, loud and warm. He had one of those truly epic laughs. It was so rare but when he let go, it was all-embracing. His eyes and his wounded spirit on song.

Said,

"See how that flies when a fucker shoves a gun in your mouth at three-thirty in the morning."

Riddle me that.

The books he was reading in those last days. As if he knew something.

Satan, your Kingdom must
    Come down . . .
                    (Massive Attack)

Playing as I perused the book titles.
"Perused."
A fifty-euro sound bite, Jack said. Adding,
"That track used in two TV series:
    Hannibal
        and
            Lecter.
The connection?
Jack's coked taste.
Those books:

    Reconstructing Amelia
    Where'd You Go, Bernadette
    Lottie Moggach, *Kiss Me First*
    Sara Gran, *The Bohemian Highway*
    Lynn S. Hightower, *Flashpoint*
    The Universe Versus Alex Woods
    Malcolm Mackay, *The Necessary Death of Lewis
        Winter*

And of course, the boxed DVDs:

    House of Cards
    Breaking Bad
    Les Revenants
    Borgen
    The Americans

And I wondered how a perpetual drunk, pill-popping, on/off nicotine freak could focus long enough for any of the above. I asked.

He said,

"Practice."

July 2013: The Galway Races on the shimmering horizon. I'd known Jack for three months. In truth, with him,

The rush.

The intensity.

The sheer hard core.

It felt like three years.

How we met? Not as you'd hazard: in a pub.

I was on the ground, my top teeth crushed by a steel-toed Dr. Martens. Two thugs, trainees almost, no more than sixteen . . . collectively had waylaid me as I came out of McDonagh's Fish 'n' Chips. Bottom of Quay Street but a bad poem away from the Spanish Arch. I was balancing my smartphone and the food, authentically wrapped in the weekly *Galway Advertiser*, the first one asked,

"Gis a chip, cunt."

The richness of Irish youth vocabulary. The second one, I'd carelessly allowed behind me.

Come on.

I'm an academic, not a kung fu fighter.

He hit me hard in my lower back with a baseball bat. The shame, not to be even mugged with authenticity, like, say, with a hurly.

Oh, America, we export too well.

Shock and pain swamped me as the first took my top teeth out with his boot. Shame too, mortification, I was taken down by . . . fuck's sake . . .

Kids!

Seriously?

Amid blood and dizziness, I gasped as both kids stood, ready to, as they chanted,

"Let's kick the fuckin be-Jaysus out of this bollix."

A figure loomed behind, then I heard,

"What's the craic?"

And he literally cracked their small, malicious skulls together. They reeled apart, moaning, and he dropped the first with a kick to the groin. He reached a hand to me, said,

"Take it slow, Pilgrim."

As . . . was I hallucinating? . . . John Wayne.

With his help, I was able to stand, even spit out some teeth. I mumbled,

"Thanks, I guess."

He smiled, said,

"A Yank."

I asked, as I tried to fight off nausea and tremors,

"Is that like . . . bad?"

He was staring at the second kid, who, though on his feet, was dazed. He answered,

"Long as you got the bucks, we love you."

Then checking my ruined mouth, said,

"Better get you to A & E."

Used his cell, called a cab, urging them,

"Get here like yesterday."

Again a faux American intonation, as if he was subtly mocking me. Sure enough, a cab screeched to a halt in, as I'd come to know Jack's term,

"Jig time."

Helped me to the cab, then turned, moved back to the seriously fucked kids, and, get this, *frisked them*.

The kid still standing, utterly dazed.

Jack slid into the seat beside me, holding the kid's money wedge, said,

"Cab fare."

Contempt
Prior
to
Investigation

From Boru Kennedy's Notes/Journals

He sees the little girl, Serena May, delighted with the new trick he showed her. How to make a silver coin disappear. He'd thought, ruefully,

A trick the banks had perfected to an inordinate degree.

The sun had been uncharacteristically hot. He'd opened the window on the first story and watched as the little girl gurgled happily on the floor.

Then he dozed.

Woken by a small cry.

Barely a whisper, more a tiny whisper of utter dread. Jumped to his feet.

The child was gone.

Thus began a whole fresh circle of hell. Later, when the full truth was revealed, he might have been partially absolved.

But forgiven?

No.

Never that.

Least of all by himself.

I worry about anyone who is lighting himself on fire for our enjoyment.

The *New York Times* wrote in 2012 about Cat Marnell, a confessional columnist who described her vampire hours, soulless sex, fragile mental state, and drug-fueled lifestyle. Her job, she said, was to be:
"Fucked up."
Jack Taylor had been doing that job all his life.

I was released from the hospital on the first day of the Galway Races. The fierce three-week heat wave had come to a deluging stop. Torrential rain lashed the streets. Did it stop the racing?

In Galway?

Like . . . hello!

A temporary bridge in my upper mouth would hold until, a cheerful doctor said,

"Some fancy dentist can charge you exorbitantly."

Dentistry, I soon learned, like everything else in Ireland, was nightmarish expensive. To my utter amazement and perhaps a little delight, my savior was standing outside the hospital's main entrance. He was wearing chinos, Crocs, and faded T-shirt with the slogan

"Is maith an talann an ocross."

(Hunger is the best sauce).

He was deeply tanned and his full head of graying hair needed a trim. Deep lines gave his face the allure of old parchment but the eyes were alive and slightly mocking. Extending a hand, he said,

"They let you out."

I took his hand, registering two missing fingers. Barely perceptible was a tiny hearing aid. I shook his hand (carefully), said,

14

"I owe you big-time."

Holding my gaze, he said,

"Jesus kid, lighten up, these are the jokes. C'mon, I'll buy you a jar."

Not for the first time I behaved like a prig, protested,

"It's not noon yet."

He sighed, took my arm, said,

"It's Race Week, the town is on the piss."

Led me across the road to a pub called the River Inn. He said,

"It's Ireland, there's not a river within spittin distance."

I noticed he limped slightly but still moved with an economy that belied his years. He was right about the town. The place was jammed but he muscled his way to the bar amid shouts of

"Taylor, thought you were dead . . ."

"Jack, ya bollix . . ."

"Lend us a tenner . . ."

"Any tips for the Plate . . ."

He ignored all, got a winning smile from the barwoman, who asked,

"Usual, Jack?"

"By two," he said,

And somehow, despite the crush, carried out a table for us by a large window. He said,

"Plant yer arse on that."

Did he mean the table? He straddled a stool, producing a second from the crowd. I sat, asked,

"How will she find us in this mob?"

He asked,

"Roisin?"

". . . if that's her name."

I trailed. He muttered,

"I hope to fuck, hell of a time to discover she's a Mary."

Then added,

"Take her a few minutes to build those pints."

"Pints!"

I said,

"Alas, not for me, Jack . . . it's Jack, yes? I'm on painkillers."

"Yah lucky fuck, the pints will have you flyin in jig time."

The woman appeared, unfazed by the madding crowd, plunked two perfect pints and two shots before us. Jack handed her a flash of notes, said,

"And one for yourself, hon."

She gave him a smile of pure radiance. He raised the pint, said,

"Slainte amach."

Downed half his pint, hammered the shot, said,

"Get that in yah, another round coming."

My Taylor baptism if not of fire, then certainly Jameson.

Flashes of
  Huge merriment
  Amazement
  Incredulity
  Pathos

16

Punctuate my fractured recollection of that first, long, insane day with Jack. We even backed a horse, named, I shit thee not:

Beckett's Boy

Ridden by A. P. McCoy

And Jack saying to me,

"See kid, the shit-hot favorite is ridden by the people's favorite,

Ruby Walsh."

He paused.

The bookies were truly like Dante's forgotten circle of a Celtic hell. Despite the ban on smoking, the air was suffused with smoke. Smoke of frenzied desperation.

Jack said,

"Bang a ton on BB."

"A ton?"

Slight shadow of annoyance flitted across his battered face, then was gone, he enunciated slowly,

"Put a hundred euros to win."

Despite the booze, the sheer adrenaline in the very air, caution whispered. I asked,

"Couldn't we, like, put fifty to show?"

Took him a moment to translate American to Irish-English, then,

"Place better? No fuckin way. I never played for safety my whole befuddled life."

I bit down, withheld,

"And gee, look at the evidence."

I played to win.

Won.

At 8 to 1.

Jesus H!

I never won a goddamn thing outside of literary stuff. I yelled,

"My Gawd, that's like, with the exchange rate, like . . . a thousand bucks!"

Tried to give him half.

No way. Jack's response . . . like this,

"Buy me dinner."

Which was chips doused in vinegar, sitting on the rocks over Galway Bay. A six-pack in a cooler and a twenty-euro dope deal.

We proceeded to:

> Do a line
> Throat-drop two fat chips
> Chug the beer

Then belch as if you meant it. With Jack, I was learning he could turn on a red cent without conversation, rhyme, or reason. He was talking about Walter Macken, veered, asked,

"How was Dublin?"

I said, of my Dublin impressions,

"What's with the rabbits?"

I told him that

(a) I was stunned by the number of beggars and in one bizarre scene, outside the ultraexpensive Brown Thomas, a man on his knees, a cardboard sign pleading for food.

(b) All the homeless guys/beggars on nigh every bridge had, get this, a rabbit.

Jack gave a resigned chuckle, said,

"Last year, on a slow news day — meaning Syria, the Banks, Household Charges were on hold — the media ran with a story of a young homeless guy who kept a pet rabbit. Some mindless morons grabbed the animal, slung it into the Liffey."

"Fuck," I said,

"Then . . ."

He continued,

"The homeless guy dived in, saved his rabbit . . . Lo and behold, he got all sorts of help, including the Mayor's Bravery Award."

Paused.

". . . so now every lowlife is trying to cash in on the act." I mulled this over, then,

"In Galway . . . are there rabbits?"

Shook his head,

"Naw, we have a no-frills gig going. Just feck the homeless guy in the river."

Impossible to tell if he was yankin my chain. I tried,

"No rabbits then?"

"Only in stew."

The
Year
of
the
Understatement

Shadow Puppets

Even now, I'm not too sure how
    Drunk
    Coked
    Crazed
    Or
None of the above Jack was when he told me about "The Man Who Tortured Women." Laid out that stark phrase like a flat hammer, turned to look at me, then,
    "Anthony de Burgo."
    Then, bitterness leaking all over his words, he sprinted,
    "Impressive name, huh? And fuck me, Tony's an impressive fellow:
    Lectures in Anglo-Irish lit, has numerous academic essays, studies, and, get this, even slums as a hack noir novelist, to, as he said on *The Late Late Show* 'pay the light bill.' Oh, Tony's a droll bollix and no mistake. Even persuaded our Galway hurlers to line out for a . . ."
    Pause,
    "Spot of cricket."
Jack took a deep breath, fired up a Marlboro Red with a heavy click of his Zippo, blew smoke, continued,

"What 'spiffin fun' that was and all for charity. The guy is a media darling. How could you not love him, too? His looks got a brooding De Niro (circa *Mean Streets*) gig going. 'Cept every few months, he grabs a teenage girl, tortures her beyond imagining, stops a breath short of murder."

Paused.

"Least so far."

Sweat had broken out above his dark eyes. He reached for the Jameson bottle, hit his coffee with it, offered, I declined, he drank deep, I asked,

"Why isn't he in jail?"

Jack seemed to shudder, then shook himself off, said,

"Tony's a clever boy, very, very, clever, and he's got the hotshots in some Rotary-type club to keep him, if not decent, certainly free."

I wasn't sure where this was going or even why he was laying it out. He saw my face, stubbed out the cig, said,

"Thing is, I'm going to take him off the board."

Was I rattled?

Phew — oh! I avoided his eyes, asked,

"Why are you telling me this? Us Americans, we specialize in euphemisms. Who else gave the English language the richness of:

bought the farm

punched his ticket

deep-sixed him?

So like, you know . . . 'take him off the board,' am I reading you correctly?"

He gave a short laugh, nodded.

24

So . . . so, I threw it out there:

"Kill him?"

Another nod.

Mystified, I reached for the bottle, poured a healthy dollop, drank, gasped, asked,

"Why on earth are you telling me?"

No hesitation.

"Because you are going to be my witness, my . . . how shall I say . . . last Will and Testament."

The Jameson singing in my blood, I near shouted,

"You gotta be . . . I mean, like, seriously, fucking kidding me."

He stood up, stretched, said,

"Kid, I never fuck around with murder."

Lines from *Literary Heroine* (Anthony de Burgo)

Everybody's fuckin dead
>of note
>perhaps . . .

Later I would learn that *Literary Heroine*, a prose
poem, was de Burgo's attempt at a "Howl-like" narrative.
Jack commented,
>"Tony likes to play, wordplay is just one facet."
Did I believe Jack was seriously going to like . . .
>>Um . . .
>>>kill a professor?
Shit,
>I mean,
>>kill anybody?
Those first head-rush, adrenalized weeks of his
company had me, to paraphrase Jack:
Be-fuddled,
Be-wildered,
Be-fucked.
As the Irish so delicately phrase it,
"I didn't know whether I was comin or goin."
My proposed treatise on Beckett was put on a
haphazard hold as I tried to find a balance in Taylor's

world. A man who was as likely to split a skull with a hurly as hand fifty euros to a homeless person (providing he didn't have a rabbit, of course).

A week after this bombshell, Jack invited me to an "Irish breakfast." We met in the GBC, Jack saying,
"The chef, Frank, he'll take care of us."
I was about to order coffee when Jack went,
"Whoa, buddy, did I not say Irish breakfast?"
". . . Um, yes."
"Right, so we're having a fry-up and, fuck me, you cannot desecrate that with coffee, it has to be tea."
I tried,
"I'm not real hot on like . . . tea."
He mimicked what the Irish think is a passable U.S. accent.
"Get with the program, pal . . ."
It wasn't . . . passable. Not even close.
Heavens to Betsy, the food came.
Thick toast with a nightmare sledge of butter,
fried eggs,
rashers,
fried tomatoes,
and, apparently, the favorite of the late pope,
black pudding.
No doubt accounting for his demise. Jack explained the cups had to be heated and he stirred the tea with gusto, said,
"This is yer real hangover antidote."
That, I truly had to take on trust. Jack ate with relish, me . . . not so much.

He asked me,
"Know the one beautiful sentence?"
Like . . . do I venture the clichés?
I love you.
I forgive you.
God loves you.
Et al. He said,
"Peace broke out."
WTF?
He smiled, briefly, said,
"Not that you need to worry, peace for us is as likely as the government cutting the country some slack. You know the latest crack? Fuckin water meters in every house. The bastards think up new ferocious schemes to hammer an already bollixed population."
I had to comment, went,
"Some turn of phrase you have there."
A shadow, no more than a whisper of rage, danced across his eyes, he asked,
"Turn of phrase? Let me give you a real beauty."
Like I had a choice.
"Lay it on me."
He intoned,
"Catholic ethos is an oily and pompous phrase . . . that sounded like a designer fragrance."
Jack reached into his jacket, pulled out a crumpled copy of the *Irish Independent* (Saturday, August 10, 2013), said,
"Here's what Liam Fay wrote:
'*Fr. Kevin Doran is a medical miracle — and indeed, a miraculous medic. He sits on the board of the Mater*

Hospital's governing body. Doran extolled the rigorous moral code underlying what he proudly calls the Catholic Ethos.'"

Jack had to pause, rein in his rage, continued,

"'In adherence to this uniquely righteous philosophy, he insisted the Mater will refuse to comply with the new law that permits abortion when a pregnant woman's life is at risk.'"

I muttered "Jesus!"

Jack put the paper aside, said,

"Whoever else is involved, it sure as shootin isn't Jesus."

I don't have a conflict of interest —
I have a conflict *and* interest.
(Phyl Kennedy-Bruen)

I'm caught staring at Jack's face. He is brutally tan, as if the sun had a vendetta, personal, and lashed him. He smiles, tiny lines, white, creaking against the parched skin, like whiteness trying to run.

He said,

"I picked up a new habit."

No need to ask if it's a good one. With Jack, all his habits are bad, very.

Continued,

"During that heat wave, I'd take half a bottle of Jay, sit on the rocks near Grattan Road, and just . . . yearn."

Back to the murder business, I asked,

"How come you know about those girls?"

Paused.

Gulp.

"And the Guards . . . don't?"

He shrugged,

"The Guards know, they just don't give a flyin fuck."

Later I Googled Father Doran and learned his areas of expertise were, as Jack would list them:

The Supernatural

      Angels

         Saints

Fairies
and
Elves.

I thought,

"Fifty shades of demonic propaganda."

Persisting,

"But you know him . . . how?"

He seemed distracted, looked around him, then snapped back, said,

"A little nun told me."

Before I could recover from this ecclesiastical bombshell, Jack said,

"Thomas H. Cook wrote in his novel *Sandrine's Case*, 'The sad thing in life is that for most people, the cavalry never arrived.'"

I managed to hold my tongue, not to be an academic asshole by saying,

"I don't read mystery novels."

I instead managed to still stay in facetious mode, remarking,

"But you're the cavalry, Jack, that it?"

Came out even more sarcastic than I intended. He let that bitter vibe hover, then,

"Most ways, son, I'm more a scalp hunter."

From Jack Taylor's Journals

Sister Maeve and I had a history, most of it convoluted, most of it bad. But a year ago, by pure luck and thuggery, I managed to return the stolen statue of Our Lady of Galway.

Back in the 1970s there'd been the phenomenon of the moving statues. Our Lady, literally seen to move in various "blessed" parts of the country, led to an almost hysterical reaffirmation of faith in the country. Quashed later by the clerical scandals. But for a brief time, there had been "Holy Ground." Our Lady of Galway had been moved by a gang of feckless teenagers.

My success in this case put me briefly back in the Church's graces.

Sister Maeve came to me, told me of two girls who'd been savagely raped and beaten, tossed aside. We'd met in Crowe's Bar in Bohermore. Sign of the fractured times in that a nun in a pub didn't raise an eyebrow, mainly because she was dressed like Meg Ryan. She'd ordered a sparkling Galway water, to see, she said,

"The tiny bubbles shimmer."

Two of her former students came to her. Amid sobs, fear, shame, and utter despair, they'd told her of their ordeal. How de Burgo, acting as mentor to their studies, had lured them to a flat on the canal. After, he'd thrown them out on the street, warning,

"Speak of this and you'll go *in* the canal." Maeve had duly reported all to her Mother Superior, who said,

"Jezebels! Common harlots who enticed a good man."

De Burgo was one of the prime movers in having extensive renovations made to the convent. Maeve, pushing aside her now flat water, said, in a very un-nun-like fashion,

"Who is going to besmirch the name of a man responsible for the central heating?"

Comfort versus truth?

No contest.

I asked Maeve,

"Why have you come to me, Sister?"

She considered her answer, then,

"Because you understand that justice is rarely delivered through ordinary channels."

Something radiantly different in a tiny, holy nun letting loose her very own

Mongrel of War.

Whatever else I thought, I didn't think she "got the right guy."

She had moral indignation, I had rage but, more important, I had the hurly.

The priest was crying.

A tear of hatred trilled down his cheek. The thin man noted it was quite lovely.

They were standing two feet apart — the man of law and the man of God.

As the tear dissolved into the thick beard, the big man wiped it away, then looked up into the thin man's eyes with loathing and slowly whispered,

"God . . . damn . . . it."

The thin man couldn't contain himself. He was grinning openly,

Was it a thrill to hear this man of the cloth taking the name of the Lord in vain?

"I knew then the bitch was mine."

(From *The Murder Room* by Michael Capuzzo)

Later, when I was asked about the essential difference between Jack,

A wild Irish fucked-up addict.

And me,

A WASP wannabe academic.

I was able to summarize it thus:

I liked to quote Beckett.

Jack quoted Joan Rivers.

And an ocean of misunderstanding flowed between the two.

Much has been said of Jack's propensity to violence. Not long after I'd found a place to rent, in Cross Street, just a drunken hen party from Quay Street, Jack announced,

"I'm treating you to dinner."

His version:

Fish 'n' chips from Supermac's on Eyre Square. It was relatively early, 7:30p.m. on a slow Galway Wednesday. Come four in the morning, when the clubs let out, it became a war zone. We were in line behind a young couple. Dressed for a night out, the guy in a smart suit, the girl in a faux power suit but without the confidence. The girl was asking,

"Please, Sean, I just want chips, no burger."

The guy's body language was flagging . . . volatile.

They got their order and the guy grabbed her portion of chips, mashed them into her suit, said,

"No burger, no fuckin eat."

I glanced at Jack, his body was relaxed, no visible sign of disturbance. For one hopeful moment, I prayed he might not even have registered the incident. We got our fish 'n' chips, then Jack added,

"A carton of your hot chili sauce."

I said nothing.

We got outside, the couple were standing at the Imperial Hotel, the guy jabbing his finger into the girl's face. Jack said,

"Give me a sec."

Ambled toward them, not a care in his stride, the chili carton oozing steam from his left hand.

He said something to the girl, who stepped back. He slapped the chili into the guy's face, gave him an almighty blow to the side of the head, asked,

"You want fries with that?"

I don't know any form that
doesn't shit on being in the most
unbearable manner.

(Samuel Beckett)

It's quite a good idea: when words fail you,
you can fall back on silence.

(Samuel Beckett)

He looked like the kind of gobshite who'd spent his
    Life
(pause)
being mildly amused.
This was Jack's verdict on a guy selling flags for
Down Syndrome Ireland. The "mildly" brought to
crushing effect the contempt he felt.
I asked Jack,
"The violence, the almost casual way you rise to it?"
He had the granite flint in his eyes, which cautioned,
"Tread very fuckin lightly."
Clicking back and forth on the Zippo, he held my
eyes, coldly said,
"For starters, you don't 'rise' but descend to
violence.
Let me paraphrase:
        'Some are born to it
        and others
        have it thrust upon them.' "
Wearying of his semantics, I asked,
"And you, which category are you?"
His eyes slid off me, dissing me curtly, said,
"Take a wild fuckin guess, hotshot."

Reaching into his battered all-weather Garda coat, he slapped a single sheet of paper before me, said,

"Read."

Four names:

Siobhan Dooley
May Feeney
Karen Brown
Mary Murphy

He said,

"All students of de Burgo."

Then abruptly standing up, he said,

"Get yer arse in gear."

"For?"

"An appointment with the eminent professor."

"What?"

"As an American high-flying student, you are meeting to discuss Beckett and the Galway Connection."

Then he shrugged, said,

"Who the fuck cares, we just want to meet the lunatic."

"We?"

He smiled, cold,

"I'm your concerned old uncle."

"Can you do 'concerned'?"

He was already moving, said,

"I can certainly do old."

★   ★   ★

The University of Galway was teeming with new prospective students. Parents in tow, they were checking out their new home. It would be the one and only time the parents got a look in. Their role from now on would be twofold:

(1) Pay for books.

(2) Pay for bail.

De Burgo's office was in the old part of the building. I noticed Jack's limp was prominent and he said,

"Gets a sympathy vote."

A secretary assured us we had to wait for only five minutes, would we like some water?

Jack said,

"With a splash of Jameson."

She gave him a look that implied:

"Old guys, they still have some moves."

Then we were told to enter Dr. de Burgo's chambers. Jack's face was granite. He looked as though he wished he still held a container of chili sauce.

De Burgo was engrossed in papers, pushed them aside with a sigh, came round the desk, hand extended, said,

"Welcome to my humble retreat."

Whatever else he implied, humility wasn't in the mix. He looked like an Ivy League professor from Central Casting. Corduroy jacket over worn plaid shirt and, yes, patches on the sleeves. Pressed navy chinos, boat shoes, a well-tended goatee below deep-set eyes. Eyes that were burning with intensity. But, as Jack would say,

"Off."

Definitely.

When he looked at you, a sense of unease slid along your spine. He motioned us to sit, then, like Mr. Laidback, perched on the edge of his desk. All was well in his academic principality. He said,

"Now Beckett, just recently I gave a lecture on the postmodern reliance of his language in relation to . . ."

Here he paused, made those air quotation marks, continued,

"The current idiom of Anglo-Irish usage."

Silence hovered.

Then Jack said,

"Cut the shit, pal."

Like a slap in the face. He turned, faced Jack, asked,

"I beg your pardon?"

Jack stood, looming over him, said,

"See this list of girls? Ring any postmodern bells?"

Shoved the four girls' names in his face. Took him a moment, then his face regrouped, he sprang from the desk, reached for the phone, said,

"I think security are needed."

Jack, unfazed, asked,

"You going to surrender to them?"

I was up, grabbing Jack's arm, said,

"We'll be leaving."

As we got to the door, Jack said,

"We'll be coming for you, fuckhead."

And I got him as far as the secretary. On her feet, she asked,

"Is everything all right?"

Jack said,

"Your boss is a serial rapist, don't be alone with him."

The critics assert that all of Beckett's characters are drawn from his early life in Dublin; the streets, bogs, ditches, dumps, and madhouses.

Beckett implied his people were the castoffs, the lunatics, the street poets, the "bleeding meat of the entire system, denizens of an urban wasteland."

I thought how well the above could easily fit Taylor's world. After our train wreck meeting with the professor, we ended up in Garavan's. They still have the snugs where you believe you have a measure of privacy. Intrusion is the theme of Jack's existence. We'd just settled with our drinks, a sparkling water for me, Jameson and the black for Jack. Jack had barely skimmed the pint's creamy head when a man burst in, plunked himself down beside Jack, gasped,

"I'm dying of thirst."

He was in his very bad fifties, wearing a distressed pin-striped suit, a grimy shirt, and blindingly white sneakers. His eyes were dancing insane reels in his head. Jack got him a pint, laid back, asked,

"What's up, Padraig?"

The man, seeing my stare, gulped half the pint, nigh shouted at me,

"Hey, I used to be someone!"

Jack muttered,

"Didn't we all?"

Another swallow and the pint was gone. He glanced at me as if I wasn't up to speed, said,

"My wife left me."
I said,
"I'm sorry."
His head cocked, question mark large in his face, he asked, amazed,
"You know her?"
Staying tight-assed polite, I said,
"No."
Spittle leaked from his lips, he near spat,
"Then why the fuck are you sorry!"
I had no answer. A light peered through his madness. He said,
"You're a Yank."
No joyriding point on this statement. I agreed I was. He turned back to Jack, offering,
"Get the fuck into Syria, help those poor fuckers."
Jack asked,
"What can I do for you, Padraig?"
His body language altered, then, positioning for the kill, he said,
"Two fifties, Jack."
The description of a hundred taking the harm/sting away. Jack gave him twenty and Padraig turned to me, asked petulantly,
"Where's your contribution?"
I shrugged.
He turned back to Jack,
"God be with the days only rich Yanks came here."
He lumbered to his feet, said,
"I'll have to go, the wife will have my dinner ready."
And he was gone, trailing bile and disappointment.

I asked,

"Did his wife come back?"

Jack gave me a look, ridicule spiced with irritation, said,

"Jesus, wake up, he never had a wife."

Needing more, I pushed,

"The pin-striped suit, was he in business?"

"Sure, if you count traffic wardens as business."

Jack indicated we were done, shucked into his all-weather coat, asked,

"Want to tag along on a case this evening?"

Gun-shy by now, I asked,

"Will there be . . . ah . . . violence?"

He gave a sly smile, said,

"We can live in hope."

A time would come when I'd tentatively ask Jack,

"Do you get a rush from . . . um . . . you know . . . the violence?"

He considered that, then,

"My friend Stewart, a Zen entrepreneur, ex-drug dealer, believed I'd become addicted to it."

He said this without rancor, it was what it was, then added,

"Like greatness, some are born to it, then others, God help them, have it thrust upon them."

I wish I'd realized what a rare moment that was. He was actually letting me in but I blew it, went the wrong way, said,

"Could you just walk away?"

Silence for a full minute, then,

"For a supposed scholar, you are as thick as two cheap lumps of wood."

Attempting recovery, I said, conciliatory,

"I'd like to meet your friend."

He laughed without a trace of humor, said,

"Good luck with that; they settled his Zen ashes across the Bay."

Daily Mail, September 2013

Headline:

250 Sex Fiends on the Run: Convicted Paedophiles and Every Hue of Sex Offender Have Disappeared or Broken the Terms of Their Release

On page 19, above a tiny paragraph, almost lost amid reports of Miley Cyrus's sexual antics, was this:

22 New Vocations to the Priesthood

Jack would ask,
"And those are connected . . ."
Pause.
"How?"

One of the rare to rarest times I was with Jack and not in a pub was over coffee in McCambridge's. Black for Jack and decaf latte for me, earning me full derision. He said,

"What's the friggin point? Without caffeine, it's like Mass without Communion; there's no hit."

I had no answer. My iPad was before me, the famous photo of Beckett as my screen saver. His face almost as lined and ruined as Jack's. I asked,

"You read Beckett?"

Gave me a long look, then,

"If I say no, you'll write me off as pig ignorant, so let me assume a literary mask and say, 'I don't read him, I savor him.'"

I nearly smiled, he said,

"Ol' Sam was a Bushmills guy."

When I didn't rise to whatever bait he was trolling, he continued,

"See, Catholics are the Jameson guys. Bushmills is for the other crowd."

He reflected on his own words, added,

"You might say black Bushmills is for . . ."

Paused.

"Black Protestants . . . and, trust me, we aren't talking about skin color."

The evening I accompanied him on "the bit of business," he was dressed in a black tracksuit, carrying an Adidas holdall. I tried to go light, said,

"Promise me there's not an AK47 in there."

"Nope, just a simple hurly."

He led me down past Spanish Arch, parked himself on a bench facing the Claddagh Basin. He motioned for me to sit. Time passed to the sound of gulls and a vague turmoil from a Quay Street hen party. Finally I asked,

"What are you waiting for?"

He nodded in the direction of a small group huddled close to an upturned boat, said,

"A fairly regular drinking school, doing no harm to anyone save themselves. Over the past few weeks, some young guy appears, drops a homemade Molotov among them. No one's been killed . . ."

He took a deep breath,

"Yet."

I had my laptop, about to open it, paused. Sounding more priggish than I intended, I said,

"Surely a case for the Guards?"

He snickered. I never actually thought there was a sound to match the word. There was. But damn it, I persisted,

"And why are you here? Indeed, why are we here?"

Lord, I sounded like a frat boy!

Jack said, in a low tone,

"They hired me."

Oh, sweet Lord, I guffawed,

And worse,

"And they'll pay you in what . . . Buckfast?"

As to what would have gone down, I'll never know, but out of the Spanish Arch shadow a man appeared, moving fast, almost a blur. His arm raised, holding a bottle, a bottle ablaze, moving toward the school. Jack was up, hurly out of the bag, and amazed me with the speed.

Whoosh!

I could hear the knee crack and the guy was down. Jack kicked the bottle aside, reached into the guy's jacket, pulled out a wallet, shoved it into his own pocket. Jack never saw the second guy, came flying from his blind side. Without even thinking I decked him with the laptop. Jack turned, said,

"No spam, eh?"

The first guy was whimpering, pleaded,

"Didn't mean no harm, just a bit of fun."

Jack said,

"You need to have that broken nose looked at."

The guy touched his unblemished nose, managed,

"What . . . ?"

As Jack swung the hurly.

We were in the bar at Jury's, it being the nearest. I was having a large Jameson to stop my trembling. Jack? He was having fun, asked,

"How's the laptop?"

"Dinged but working."

He raised his glass, said,

"Like the mighty fool."

He flipped through the guy's wallet, saying,

"This kid likes cash."

Three hundred euros. Then a driver's licence, he read,

"Owen Liffey. The fuck is named after a river and worse, a Dublin river."

I could feel the drink warming me, even starting a buzz. As if reading me, Jack said,

"It's why we drink it, kid."

Then he suddenly whirled around, his eyes traveling the length of the bar, an odd expression lighting his face. I asked,

54

"Seeing a ghost?"

He turned back, said,

"Yeah, sort of. I was only ever in here once. I was laden with a case, *The Killing of the Tinkers*. I wanted some downtime, a pub where I knew no one."

He gave a brief laugh, then,

"Who am I going to know drinks at Jury's — Chris de Burgh? There was a guy, right at the end of the bar, sinking what I think you call boilermakers."

"Sure, a shot and a brew."

His eyes flashed, he asked,

"Did I ask you for a definition? I know what the fuck it is. You have yet to learn the one essential mode of Irish survival."

I shot,

"Always buy your round?"

He sighed, said,

"Never under any circumstances *interrupt* a story!"

A few tense moments followed, then he resumed,

"The guy was a take-no-prisoners drinker. Serious, sure, methodical. I'm not sure how, but we got talking. He'd spent time in a jail in South America . . . Like an eejit, I said, 'Well, least you got back.' The guy stood up, gave me one of those looks that plays a reel on your soul, said, 'It's what I brought back with me that's the worry.'"

I waited until I was sure he was finished, asked,

"Did he mean he picked up some . . . like, disease?"

"Only if the soul can be afflicted."

Outside, I was saying good night when Jack handed me the three hundred euros, said,

"Give it to the drinking school."
Whoa, hold the goddamn phones. I asked,
"Why don't you?"
He was moving away toward the water, said,
"I don't want to encourage them."

I didn't see him for a week. I'd moved into a small apartment in Lower Salthill. The rent was about the same as the national debt. I was still hamstrung between my Beckett dissertation and a book on Jack. Something about Galway had seeped into my bones and I almost felt that I belonged. I was brewing coffee, arranging my papers on a small table when the bell went. Opened the door to Jack, he said,
"I bring gifts."
I asked,
"How did you find me?"
"The postman told me."
I was outraged, asked,
"Are they allowed to do that?"
He raised his eyes, said,
"Jaysus, lighten up . . . are you askin me in?"
I stepped aside.
He handed me a bottle of Jameson and a cross which seemed to be made of reeds. He said,
"Saint Bridget's Cross, keep your home safe."
I was moved, covered with,
"Does it work?"
He sat in my only armchair, said,
"Time ago I gave a home owner a solid silver cross. A burglar buried it in his chest."

56

Where do you go with such a tale? I went to my excuse of a kitchen for the two mugs I owned. One had the logo "667."

I handed it to Jack, who said,

"I get it, the neighbor of the beast."

He uncapped the Jay, poured lethal amounts. I said,

"I'll get some water."

He growled,

"Water this and I'll break your neck."

Skipped the water.

Jack knocked his back, said,

"Slainte amach,"

I sipped mine. He looked around, said,

"Need to get Vinnie here, from Charley Byrne's Bookshop, furnish the place."

I said,

"I have a Kindle."

"And may God forgive you."

It was a few days later, I decided to drop the dime on Jack. To, as the Brits say, "grass him up."

To be what Jack would have spat,

"A treacherous informer."

The scourge, no less he claimed, of Irish history.

Syria continued to be torn asunder by Assad. Despite repeated evidence of the use of chemical weapons against the rebels, the world dithered and demurred. Obama condemned the regime but still took no military action. The United Kingdom voted against intervention. Syria burned alone.

Niall Horan of One Direction reached the Rich List. This news pushed Syria from the front pages. It was not difficult to understand Jack's lament,

"Nobody gives a tuppenny fuck."

By reporting his projected threat against de Burgo, I felt I was at least trying to give "a good goddamn."

. . . his unshaved head and unwashed look
Made me think of a man who has gone into
another country. One where a person can be
dissolute without penalty, only to return home
and find everything he owns in ruins.

    (*Light of the World* by James Lee Burke)

I made an appointment to meet with the top guy, Superintendent Clancy. He'd recently been named

Super Cop

and won the highest award the precinct can bestow on a Guard.

A sad irony that he had once been Jack's best buddy. They'd trained together at Templemore, been holy terrors on the hurling field, and always

"had each other's back"

until

Jack's drinking had him disgracefully bounced from the force while Clancy climbed the ranks, awash in glory.

Over the years they'd become bitter enemies. The golden friendship steeped in envy and bitterness. Who ever thought he'd save Jack from the fatal action he was planning? It had, if you will, a poetic symmetry.

I met the super on a Monday morning. An air of gloom pervaded the Garda station as Ireland had just lost one-nil to Austria, shattering any slim hope of World Cup qualification. The manager, an aging Italian, Giovanni Trappatoni, had resigned. Over five years he'd received ten million! Read it and weep.

Plus, a golden handshake of 500,000 euros. His tenure, according to Jack,

"Reached a new low in Irish soccer."

I was led into the super's office by a tank of a Guard who had, he said,

"A sister in Boston."

He didn't ask if I knew her but it was there, hovering. Over and over in Ireland, I'd had this experience and saw the look of incredulity when I didn't know the aunt, niece, brother in just about any state of the union.

Clancy was behind a massive oak desk, strewn with files and papers. Dressed in full blue, he had a riot of decorations on the tunic. A big man, swollen even larger by good living, but with a brute force emanating, cautioned,

"Don't mistake flab for weakness."

He stood up, extended a huge meaty hand, said,

"Always glad to welcome a Yank."

Then to the other Guard,

"Tea for our visitor or would you prefer coffee? We even home-brew the best Colombian."

And he waited.

I realized this was a joke and, a little behind, tried a smile, said,

"I'm good, thank you."

His eyes crinkled and, to my horror, I realized more humor was coming.

He said,

"Better be good or we'll feel your collar."

62

He came around the desk, gave me a resounding thump on the back, said,

"Just kidding. Sit your arse down and let me know how I can be of service."

I was beginning to veer toward Jack's antipathy. I said,

"Um, it's a little delicate and may even sound far-fetched."

He hovered over me, boomed,

"Trust me, lad, we've heard it all here, so spill . . ."

And, alas, spill I did.

All.

The very mention of Jack had him on high alert. He listened without interruption until the whole sad, sordid saga was spent.

Moved back behind his desk, put his size twelves on the desk, said,

"Taylor is a drunk, a fabulist, he even believes some of his own fantasies. Much as I'd like your . . ."

Pause.

"Yarn to be true, it's horseshite. Even Taylor, with all his dodgy dealings and, dare I say, nefarious enterprises, not even he would quite stoop to such a lunatic scheme."

He stood up.

I was being dismissed and, hate to admit, shamed. My cheeks burned. Clancy said,

"And let's face it, sonny, if you're his friend, he's even more bollixed than I thought. But, tell you what, if you ever get something solid — like date, time, location, give us a call. We live to serve."

I'd gotten to the door, feeling as crushed as a Beckett character in a garbage bin, when Clancy said,

"If you intend to reside a while . . ."

He let contempt pour over that word, then,

"It might behoove you to remember that we tolerate most shenanigans on this proud little island of ours but . . ."

He stared me full in the face,

"But we fucking loathe informers."

Later that day, a female Guard named Ridge, recently returned to the force after a horrendous accident, dropped the dime on me. To Jack!

It is biologically impossible for a human being to remain conscious in the face of such a potent weapon of narcolepsy as a modern . . . politician. Boring, snoring, Rachel Reeves isn't the only dull MP.

(Stephen Pollard, editor of *The Jewish Chronicle*)

Even if you're a brain surgeon, you're allowed to be interested in your appearance.

(Alexandra Shulman, editor in chief of British *Vogue*, reassures women that it's all right to be clever and talk about frocks)

When I'd ventured to Jack my idea of writing about him, he said,

"Jesus, get a fuckin life."

Undeterred, I continued and carefully (very), I'd ask him questions. He snapped,

"I don't do sharing."

But somewhere in there, he wasn't entirely resistant. Sometime later, he said,

"Perhaps you could do a Tom Waits."

Lost me.

I said,

"Lost me."

He sighed, said,

"For a young guy, part of the most sophisticated techno-savvy generation, you are pig ignorant of the things that matter."

Annoyed, I tried,

"And like . . . Tom . . . whoever . . . matters?"

He was shaking his head.

"Fuck me, that's like asking if the Clash are relevant."

I sat down, waited, then got,

"Tom Waits said,

'Shall I tell you the truth or just string
You along?'"
Getting no comment from me, he went on,
"I like the idea of the unreliable narrator."
Why was I not surprised?

That evening a book dropped through my mailbox.
Patricia Highsmith, *Edith's Diary*.
A note enclosed:
Kid,
    About the best unreliable narrator you could read.
Maybe pick up a few pointers.
                                              J.T.
Was he asking/telling me a lie?

After my visit to Superintendent Clancy — I'm not
going to lie to you — I felt bad, real shitty. I'd not only
done a pretty dubious act but damn, it had blown up in
my face. Clancy had not only dismissed me but oh,
Lord, effectively called me a rat, a fink.

I took the Jack solution, I went to a bar, Jury's, and
who knows, maybe I thought I might run into the
South American specter. The bar was pretty much
empty, mirroring accurately how I felt.

Two young women were at a corner table poring over
a magazine. I ordered a 7 and 7 and got a look from the
bar guy.

"Seagram's 7 and 7-Up."

His look said . . . "Then, that's what you should have
said."

Day just kept giving!

I was considering a second one when a voice said,
"Oh, go on, live a bit."
One of the girls ordering wine spritzers. I noticed how pretty she was, verging on seriously hot.
Because I'd been around Jack his, shall I say, "terseness" rather than "blunt rudeness" had rubbed off.
I snapped,
"How would it be if you minded your own business."
A beat.
Then,
She laughed out loud, said,
"A guy with balls. You're a rare breed."
I sank back into my funk. Twenty dire minutes later, I finished the drink and, if anything, it had deepened my despair. Asked myself if it was too late to get back on my Beckett or cut my literary loss, head stateside. On the way to the door, the girl blocked my path. And her looks? She could be a ringer for Meadow, Tony Soprano's daughter and, in my fragmented book, that was solid. She asked,
"Are you some kind of mature student?"
Mature was imbued with a weight of scorn.
I tried for Jack's "wipe the floor" with her but I had nothing. Her face, just truly lovely, had unnerved me. She stood there for a moment assessing me.
Man, there are few analyses like that of an Irishwoman. It's not even so much what you are as
"what they might make of you."
Scary shit.
She asked,

"If I marry you will I get a green card?"
I spluttered,
"What the . . ."
She gave a radiant smile, said,
"But let's play by the rules. Meet me here at eight tomorrow and buy me dinner."
I managed,
"Like a date?"
She was turning on her heel, then,
"Well, it's hardly like a . . . tragedy."

A shopping mall in Nairobi was seized by terrorists brandishing automatic weapons. They screamed at anyone who was a Muslim to leave. A young non-Muslim, an Englishman, managed a few nervous words of Arabic and was released. They then began to systematically murder the remainder. At least fifty people were killed.

My dinner date with Aine (it was, she said, Irish for Ann) went well. After I asked her to my apartment for a coffee, she said,
"You just want a fuck."
Good Lord!
Then she added,
"Let's see if you're worth screwing."
I thought her use of the most basic obscenity was a test and, heavens to Betsy, it certainly was testing, but I felt I could hang in there. Bottom line being that she kept me off balance and that in itself was a rush. She said to me,

"If a man says no to a woman, she wants to die. If a woman says no to a man, he wants to kill."

I told her a partial truth, said,

"That's very provocative."

And got that Irish look, mix of amusement and derision, as she answered,

"But provocative to whom?"

Van Veeteren assumed that in this simple
way he was obtaining permission to proceed
from a higher authority and wondered
in passing if this might be one of the motives
for all religious activities: the need to pass responsibility
on to someone else.
(Håkan Nesser, *The Strangler's Honeymoon*)

I was attempting to explain to Aine why I'd started writing a book on Jack Taylor, began with,

"The guy saved my ass."

She was skeptical, said,

"He stopped a street fight! It hardly merits you devoting your life to him."

As I've said, Aine was hot but, truth to tell, exasperating. I continued,

"One book is hardly devotion."

She fixed on me that intense no-prisoners Irish gaze,

"You got some high-flying scholarship to study Samuel Beckett and you're jeopardizing that to write about a worn-out alky nobody?"

I tried to explain that mystery and Ireland would be a surefire combination in the States. Then I could, having sold film rights, return to Beckett at my leisure. She was raging.

"Are you three kinds of eejit! A book about a broken-down Kojak in the west of Ireland is going to fly?"

I said, rattled,

"I know about books."

She rolled her eyes, said,

"And sweet fuck-all about the real world."

★ ★ ★

A single entry in Jack Taylor's journal/notes for all of September 2013:

"Cuir fidh se anois a chuid gaoither anois"

(Now it shall please his conscience now).

Jack's TV viewing had once been a learning curve all of itself. He asserted that American television was the new literature, that the finest writing was contained in the scripts of

Breaking Bad
Game of Thrones
Low Winter Sun

reaching back to *The Sopranos* and excelling onward. But like the darker turn in his psyche, he was now enthralled by

Hardcore Pawn

A pawnshop set in the middle of Detroit's 8 Mile, it was *Jerry Springer* meets *American Horror Story*.

Pawnshops, he said,

"We're the new Church of Ultimate Despair."

Kennels for the Hound of Heaven.

A linguistics expert has predicted
that the next generation of young Irish
people will speak with American accents.

I was treating Aine to dinner in Fat Freddy's in Quay Street. They do a seriously good chili. Aine was having coq au vin, smiling as she said it to me,

"Irish people can never order that with a straight face."

We'd just started a carafe of the house wine when I excused myself to answer my cell. Took the call outside on the street amid a riot of hen parties and young people celebrating exam results. The call was from my former tutor in Dublin, who, no frills, asked,

"The fuck are you playing at?"

Meaning, my abandonment of my tenure at Trinity as part of my scholarship.

I lied, said,

"Just taking time out to savor the country."

Pause, then,

"Savor fast and get your arse back here, you don't want to lose your place."

Lots of replies to this but I went with brown-nosing,

"Yes, sir, I'll be back in a few weeks."

Buying time if not affection.

When I returned to the table, a man was sitting in my chair, leaning across the table, apparently engrossed in conversation. I went,

"What the hell . . . ?"

The man stood up, mega smile, hand out, said,

"Boru, forgive me. I was just keeping your lovely lady company."

Something in the way he said "lovely" leaked a creepy familiarity over the word and I realized who he was:

The professor, de Burgo.

As I put this in some kind of skewed perspective, he rushed,

"I spotted you earlier and just wanted to pop over, ask if there was a chance you'd guest-lecture for my department."

He then literally ushered me into my chair, handed me a business card, said,

"But let me not spoil your evening. Give me a bell when you get a chance and, truly, we'd be delighted to have you on board."

And he was gone.

He looked old, like a stranger.
He was someone else, someone whom
he could easily hate.
(Tom Pitts, *Piggyback*)

Jack seemed to get his rocks off on subtly putting me down.

Well, maybe not so subtly.

He'd been telling me of the golden age of TV, when he was a young man, said,

"Fuck, we had *Barney Miller* and the magnificent *Rockford Files*."

I admitted that, no, I didn't know those shows. He said,

"And you'll look back on what? The Kardashians!"

I went the wrong tack, tried,

"I don't really watch a lot of television."

And he was off.

Like this,

"Course not, you're too freaking academic to slum, you probably have wet dreams about Kurosawa and Werner Herzog."

Jesus!

I said,

"That is reverse elitism."

He laughed out loud, said,

"Bet you're one of those pricks who say, 'I don't read fiction,' then sneak into the toilet with the *National Enquirer*."

★ ★ ★

The Irish people were going to the polls, a referendum on two points:

(a) To keep or abolish the senate.

(b) To set up a new court of appeals.

A fast track for cases in reality.

Jack was shucking into his all-weather Garda coat. I asked,

"You have to be somewhere?"

He stared at me, said,

"I'm going to vote."

I was astounded, said,

"You . . . you vote?"

And he looked as if he might deck me, asked,

"You think alkies don't have rights, that it?"

In exasperation, I said,

"There's no talking to you."

"No, you mean there's no *lecturing* me!"

A day later I was having a drink with Aine. We were in Hosty's, early in the evening, and a nice air of quiet pervaded. I'd nearly perfected the pronunciation of her name, had it as close to

"Yawn-ah."

Without the "y," obviously.

We were doing well, she was telling me about a beauty course she was close to finishing. Then, she hoped to open a nail salon. I asked,

"There's money in nails?"

And got the look.

The door behind me banged open but I didn't turn around. Then a hand grabbed my collar, hauled me off the stool. I crashed to the floor, my pint spilling over a new white shirt I was sporting. Jack stood over me, his fists balled, spit flying from his mouth, he rasped,

"You tout, you piece of treacherous shit, you ratted me out to the Guards . . ."

He had to pause for breath, some control, then,

"And to Clancy, fucking Clancy of all people!"

Aine was trying to grab Jack, pull him back, but he effortlessly shrugged her away, said,

"I thought we had some kind of friendship! If you were anybody else, I'd kick your fucking head in."

Aine shouted,

"Leave him alone. I'll call the Guards!"

He turned to her and the manic rage seemed to ebb. He said,

"Jesus, the Guards! You two deserve each other."

He looked down at me, said,

"You sorry excuse for a man."

And then threw some notes onto the counter, said to the stunned barman,

"Buy these two beauts a drink, something yellow, And weak as piss."

I would prefer to be in a coma
and just be woken up and wheeled
out onstage and play and then put back
in my own little world.
(Kurt Cobain)

It was Aine who declared,

"OK, if you're going to do a book on that . . ."

She faltered,

"Asshole,"

Then,

"You're going to have to be the scholar we keep hearing you are."

I wasn't sure where this was going, said,

"Not sure where this is going."

She stifled her impatience, explained,

"Sources . . . research, talk to the people who know/knew him."

Made sense.

Within a few days I had a list.

Like this,

Assorted barpersons.

A woman named Ann Henderson, supposedly the one and only great love of his life. Of course, as used in Taylorland, the affair had ended badly with Ann marrying another Guard, an archenemy of Jack. Indeed, it was hard to find people who weren't enemies of his, arch or otherwise.

Cathy and Jeff, the parents of the Down syndrome child whose death was widely attributed to Jack's negligence.

Ban Garda Ridge, a sometime accomplice, confidante, and conspirator of Jack's.

Father Malachy. A close friend of Jack's late mother and someone who'd known Jack for over twenty years. I was hoping he'd shed some light on Jack's hard-on for the Church. In light of the recent clerical scandals, maybe *hard-on* was a poor choice of noun.

A solicitor who'd haphazardly dealt with Jack's numerous escapades with the Guards.

There was a Romanian, Caz, whose name featured often but he'd apparently been deported in one of the government sweeps.

The Tinkers were among the few who held Jack in some sort of ethnic regard.

Father Malachy was the parish priest at St. Patrick's, the church of note for Bohermore. I had called ahead and, on arrival, was met by a nun. She was so old that she was practically bent in two. I wasn't sure if I should acknowledge her physique and stoop to her level. Jack would have said we'd bent down enough for the Church. She raised a feeble arm, pointed, said,

"The Father is in the sacristy."

I tried,

"I don't wish to disturb him."

In a surprisingly terse tone, she snapped,

"Ary, he's been disturbed for years."

Then declared,

"You're a Yank!"

"Um . . . yes."

"I have a sister in San Francisco, with the Sisters of the Pure of Heart."

Wow, so many ways to play with that line. But she asked,

"Did you bring something?"

. . . Just an attitude . . .

I said,

"No, should I have?"

"And they say Yanks are flaithiúil (generous)."

I headed down the aisle and she fired,

"You're already on the wrong foot."

Every day is a gift . . .
but does it have to be a
pair of socks?

(Tony Soprano)

Father Malachy was almost invisible behind a cloud. The effect was startling, as if a Stephen King fog or mist had enshrouded him. Then the stale fetid smell of nicotine hit like a hammer. He was in his late fifties, with a face mottled by rosacea, broken veins, and what I guess can only be described as lumps. He was dressed in clerical black, dandruff like a shroud on his shoulders. And I have to be mistaken, but the magazine he wiped off the cluttered desk seemed a lot like the *National Enquirer*.

Surely not?

He peered at me, rheumy-like, and, with not one hint of compassion, he snapped,

"What'd you want?"

I said,

"I'm Boru Kennedy and wonder if I might have a . . ."

He barked,

"What the shite kind of name is that? Are ya a Yank?"

I'd seen *The Quiet Man* and *Darby O'Gill and the Little People*, but any Hollywood image of the jovial Irish priest bore no relation to this ogre. Luckily, I had been cautioned to bring a bottle. To, as Aine suggested, "wet his whistle."

Not sure why I told the nun I had nothing but Jack had advised me once . . . Lie always to the clergy, it is their stock-in-trade.

I handed over the bottle.

Jameson, of course.

I was a dude who learned.

If he was grateful, he gave no sign. He growled,

"I've a cousin in the Bronx. He works for the Sanitation Department."

Then he laughed,

"The bollix is down the toilet."

Pause, another cig, then,

"What do you want?"

I took a deep breath, lied,

"I'm doing a profile of . . . um . . . colorful Galway personalities and I wonder if you might, please, have some thoughts on the ex-policeman Jack Taylor?"

I waited for an explosion, a torrent of abuse, but a sly grin danced along his lips, he asked,

"How much are you paying?"

Of course.

In my time in Ireland, I'd learned a few moves for dealing with the locals:

(1) Never . . . ever, pump yourself up.
(2) Adopt a nigh manic love of hurling. You didn't have to actually learn the game, just mutter "Ah, will we ever see the likes of D.J. Carey again?"
(3) Make almost undetected snide comments on

non-nationals, sliding in mention of the Holy
Grail, i.e., medical cards.

(4) Constantly refer to the weather as simply *fierce*.

(5) Buy the first round but especially the last.

(6) Rile a priest to get him going.

I went with number 6, said,

"They say Jack saved your life."

Phew!

Fireworks.

He was on his feet, cigarette smoke nigh blinding
him, spittle leaking from his mouth. He shouted,

"That whore's ghost of a bollix! He killed a child and
don't even get me started on how he drove his saint of
a mother into an early grave."

He blessed himself, adding,

"May she rest in the arms of Jesus, the Bed of
Heaven to her."

Lest he launch into a full-blown rosary, I tried,

"I was told the child's death was an accident."

He made his *hmph* sound, underwrit with
indignation, said,

"Ask her parents, yeah, ask them if it was an
accident."

He was eyeing the bottle, could only be moments
before he climbed in and that was an event I wished to
bear witness to. But he changed tack, said,

"Our new pope, supposedly he's embracing the
simple life. No Gucci slippers for him."

He fumed on that a bit, then conceded,

"Least he sacked that bishop who just built a thirty-one-million place."

Threw his arms out to embrace his run of his home, said,

"And they expect me to live on the charity of the parish! You know how much they put in the basket at Mass last Sunday?"

I was guessing, not a lot.

"Twenty-four euros, two buttons, and a scratch card."

The urge to ask if he won. On the card.

I stood up to take my leave, said, offering my hand,

"Thank you so much for your time."

But he was still in hate-Taylor mode, didn't quite know how to turn it off. He asked,

"You heard about him and the nun?"

Sounded like the title of a very crude joke. I tried,

"I do know he's close to Sister Marie."

He shot me a look of contemptible pity, spat,

"Not that wannabe Mother Teresa. Years ago he was working on a case involving a murdered priest and an old frail nun had been working with the poor murdered fellah. Taylor said to her . . ."

Pause.

"I hope you burn in hell."

I had an ace, played,

"Wasn't that the time Jack saved you from serious child abuse allegations?"

We were done.

On his feet, he snarled,

"Get out of my office . . . ya . . ."

He searched for the most withering insult and as I reached the door, he trumpeted,

"Yah Protestant."

That evening I had dinner with Aine and related the encounter with the priest. She said,

"There was a time, you know, priests ruled the roost here."

I thought how far they'd tumbled, said,

"Seems like they're reduced to scraping the bottom of the Irish barrel."

She laughed, said,

"More like these days, it's shooting clerical fish in the barrel."

I'd been spending more and more time with her and, I don't know about love, but it had certainly moved into an area of need. We had grappa with the after-dinner coffee and she smiled, said,

"Lucky you."

Being with her, having found her, I felt way more than lucky but I asked,

"Why?"

That malicious twinkle in her eye, she said,

"I know for a fact you're getting laid."

Notes from Boru's Papers
The days slipped by,
the hate remains.
(Jens Lapidus,
Easy Money)

Amen

To that, Jack thought.

He had spoken again to Sister Maeve. One of the girls allegedly attacked by de Burgo had killed herself. Left a note for Sister Maeve.

It read:

I feel so dirty, so defiled.
  My priest says I am a liar.
  Please pray for my tainted soul.

Like a haiku of bitter acid. Etched in utter despair. Jack pledged,

"If it's my last act, I'll make that bastard burn."

Took me a time to track down Ann Henderson. She was, according to most sources, the "love of Jack's life."

She had some colorful, varied history her ownself. After Jack, she had married a Guard. This same individual for various motives decided Jack needed

"the lesson of the hurly."

A very Galway practice. Involving three ingredients:

(1) A knee
(2) A hurly
(3) Rage

Took out Jack in one lethal swoosh, leaving him with a permanent limp. As stories go, this would be sufficiently dark, adequately noir for the most jaded palate. But in Taylorland, half measures availed them nothing. A vigilante group, named the Pikemen, in a misguided attempt to recruit Jack, took out the hurler.

Ann blamed Jack.

It wasn't then that they had simply history, it was open brutal wafare.

Jack lost . . . as always.

I met Ann at the Meryck Hotel. On the phone she said,

"Let's pretend we have some class."

Irishwomen had this lock on non sequiturs. Did they always have the last word? According to Jack, they most certainly always had the last laugh, regardless of how bitter. I'm not sure what I was expecting. An aging woman, gray and broken from grief and her legacy of men, downtrodden?

I think that was the description I was anticipating.

Quelle surprise . . . which Jack had Irish-translated as "Fuck me sideways!"

She was well groomed, finely preserved, indeterminate forty-through-fifty range. An immaculate tailored navy coat, strong face, with that melancholic slant that attracted rather than repelled. Her hair was shot through with blond highlights. The eyes, intense blue with a light that spoke of deep reserves. She welcomed me warmly, said,

"But you're little more than a gasun."

The pat-your-head, kick-your-ass sandwich her nation specialized in.

We ordered tea. Yeah, I was trying to go native. Was even managing to swear without consciously thinking about it. She asked,

"So, how can I help you?"

I launched. Gave her most of my Taylor narrative. She was a good listener. Took a time but eventually I was done. Not sure what responses I was anticipating but laughter wasn't among them. She said,

"You need to watch that."

"What?"

I'd deliberately avoided cusswords. She gave me a warm smile, and how it lit up her face. I could see how Jack would have cherished its glow. She said,

"I could be listening to Jack."

She had to be kidding. I tried,

"You have to be kidding."

She reached over, touched my arm, said,

"You have taken on his speech patterns. Next you'll be making lists."

Clumsily, I tried to cover the current list with my teacup. She continued,

"Jack has a dark, very dark magnetism. Alas, it obliterates those who stay drawn to it. Look at his closest friends . . . Stewart,"

Pause.

Dead.

Then,

"Ridge . . . just out of hospital. Not to mention a long line of casual acquaintances, bartenders, street people, so-called snitches, even an innocent child. All Taylor-tainted and all dead or wounded. My own husband and, God forgive me, my own lost heart."

Fuck!

I noticed she still wore the Irish wedding band, the Claddagh ring. The heart turned inward — for whom, Jack or her husband?

I didn't ask.

Did ask,

"Do you hate him?"

She seemed quite astonished, took a moment to regroup, then,

"Not so long ago it seemed as if Jack might be on the verge of happiness."

We both laughed nervously at such a notion. She continued,

"An American he met on a weekend in London. The affair apparently burned bright and rapidly. The high point was her impending visit to Galway . . . Jack was aglow."

I went,

"Wow, hold the phones. She knew about his drinking, right?"

She rolled her eyes, said,

"Mother of God, everybody and his sister knows that! There was another woman, hell-bent on destroying every aspect of Jack's life and had somehow gotten hold of his mobile. The American arrived, no one to meet her at the airport, so . . ."

She took a deep breath.

"She answered Jack's phone, said,
'Jack can't come to the phone,
he's about to come in me.' "

I went Irish,

"Holy fuck!"

I ventured,

"Do you still have some . . . um . . . residual feelings for Jack?"

She laughed but not with any warmth, said,

"Residual! Jesus, sounds like a TV repeat. How deeply fucked is the ordinary art of conversation by political correctness."

Her use of obscenity gave her words a blunt trauma and also affirmed that this line of questioning was done. She gathered her coat, asked,

"What happened to your friendship with the bold Jack?"

Taken aback, I considered some answers that might put me in a better light. This woman's approval seemed necessary. I said simply,

"I betrayed him."

She took a sharp breath, then,

"Phew, that's bad, no return there."

I asked,

"He doesn't forgive betrayal?"

"Jack doesn't forgive anything or anyone."

I reverted to American, said,

"Hard-core, eh?"

She gave me a look, savored that, said,

"There is one person he can never forgive."

I wanted to guess, "Your husband," but some discretion held my tongue. She had such a look of profound sadness, so I asked,

"Who might that be?"

"Himself."

Those who actually work say
"I get wages."
Those who just think they work say
"I'm on a salary."
(Jack Taylor)

Jack had recently resumed drinking in the River Inn. He hung there as NUIG staff like to unwind near the university. After a grueling day of between one and two lectures. One guy dressed in a worn cord jacket with, and I kid thee not, patches on the elbows, was a regular. A man who'd read his John Cheever or watched one too many episodes of *University Challenge*. He liked to drink large Jamesons, no ice, no water. A dedicated souse. Jack knew him slightly from Charley Byrne's bookshop, where he spent hours loitering in the Literary Crit section.

Jack began to join him at the counter, freely buying him rounds, creating an artificial camaraderie through drink. The guy liked to talk a lot.

A few sessions in, Jack slipped de Burgo into the chat, began,

"Professor de Burgo seems to be highly respected."

No one pisses on academics like their colleagues. The guy didn't disappoint, muttered,

"Cock of the fucking English Department."

Gently prodding, needling, Jack brought the prey to play, said,

"A firm favorite of the ladies, I hear."

113

Bingo!

The torrent opened, accompanied by a huge "umph."

"Ladies' man, my arse. He lines up all the naive starry-eyed first-year students, grooms them, and then . . . in his words . . ."

He took a hefty belt of the Jay, as if what was coming needed lubrication, certainly artificial strength, said,

"Nails the cunts."

Jack bit back his own ice-cold fury, asked quietly,

"How does he get away with it?"

No hesitation.

"Connected. The Garda super, half the city's movers and shakers, they're his golf buddies."

Jack wondered how much he could reveal of what Sister Maeve had told him of the condition of the girls, went with,

"I've been told those girls are in a bad way."

He nodded ruefully, said,

"Time back, I'd a bottle of Old Midleton, a real fine vintage, got buried into it with the professor, and recklessly observed, 'Jesus, you could kill one of those girls.'"

Jack said,

"Bet that rattled him."

He glanced up at the TV. Sky News was reporting on 25,000 lost in the Philippines typhoon. Some horrors are of such magnitude you can't grasp them. He shook his head, seeing but not assimilating. He said,

"De Burgo laughed, said, 'One can always dream.'"

114

Then he abruptly stood, glared as if Jack stole something from him, said,

"I don't think I want to talk to you anymore."

Jack sat for a time, his mind careering amid nails, typhoons, and stray snatches of conversation from other drinkers. Their main topic was the appointment of Martin O'Neill as Ireland's new manager with the red-hot announcement of his assistant, Roy Keane.

Keane was a tornado of a whole different caliber. The government was pleased, took the spotlight off its cancellation of medical cards for children with Down syndrome. Jack ordered another pint, watched the slow build of the black, and thanked some deity for at least one unchanged staple.

Next on my list of Taylor trails was Ban Garda Ni Iomaire. Female Guard Ridge. Now a sergeant, she'd only recently returned to duty after a horrific accident. My data were meager. She was gay, combative, and once a close Taylor ally.

Now, she was simply elusive. I'd left messages, called the station, and hit a brick wall. Finally it was Aine who tracked her down. They attended the same gym. She agreed to meet me in Java coffee shop. I'm not sure what I expected. A woman who not only survives in the Guards but gets promoted, well, she was hardly going to be a shrinking violet.

The first surprise was her size; she was small, almost petite. She moved with a grace due perhaps to her kickboxing training. A large gash across her forehead testified to the gravity of her recent accident. I was sitting and rose as she approached. She snapped,

"Spare me the gallant shite."

Oh, boy!

She sat, leveled hard brown eyes on me, asked,

"You a Jack fan?"

I stammered,

"Um . . ."

She ordered,

"You pushed to meet me and now what, you're shy? Jesus!"

Oh, Lord, another ballbuster. I decided on diplomacy, asked,

"How are you after the accident?"

Big, big mistake.

"Accident! Do you know me? No, so why would you give a toss as to how I am or do you mean the train wreck that is Taylor?"

It was probably too late to run. So, haltingly I told her of my project, the book on Jack and my plan to interview those who know him.

She appeared to be only half-listening as she ordered herbal tea. The waitress was having some difficulty with this, asked,

"You do know this is called Java? The hint is in the name, meaning, 'Hello?' We serve coffee."

Before this escalated, I put in my two cents, said,

"Chamomile is good."

No kidding, they both glared at me. Ridge said,

"You hear anybody ask you?"

Maybe they were sisters! Certainly related in animosity. We waited until her tea came, she didn't touch it, just fixed me with that stare, the one that says,

"Let's hear it, asshole."

I asked,

"How would you describe Jack?"

"A feckless drunk."

OK.

I waited.

Nothing further.

I tried,

"But he did have a certain measure of success. I mean . . . with your assistance of course."

She rolled her eyes, then,

"Cases got solved despite him, not because of him."

I felt frustration building but strove for an even tone, asked,

"So why did you hang in there all these years?"

Her body language altered, not a lot but a modicum less of steel. Maybe chamomile is underrated. She said,

"Time was, I thought the light shone stronger in Jack than the darkness. I believed he was running from the ugliness, the brutality. But I was wrong. All the time, he was courting it until finally it became not a part of him but all of him."

I said,

"Wow, that's a bleak picture."

She was done, stood up, said,

"He's a bleak man."

Desperate, I asked,

"Surely there is at least one redeeming feature?"

She seemed to consider that, then,

"He knows who he is. If that's a point in his favor, then he's even more fucked than I've said."

She had reached the door when a thought hit her. She came back, leaned over the table, got right in my face. She was proof that sheer physical intimidation has less to do with build than intent. She said,

"You want, as you Yanks say . . ."

hissed this,

". . . a sound bite?"

She let me taste that, then,

"A blurb, isn't that what they call them? Hell, you could even use it as a title, Jack Taylor is

      a

        Spit

          in

            the

              Face."

Then she was gone.

I wiped at my face as if spittle had landed there.

The only difference between
a rut and a grave
is the dimensions.
(Jack Taylor)

Aine was hugely excited, called me to say we had to meet, she had great news.

OK?

We meet in Crowe's, she ordered a vodka, slimline tonic. I had a pint of Smithwick's. I loved Guinness but, oh man, that sucker sits in your gut like lead. She looked, oh, my God, so darn pretty, and all lit up, gave a glow to eyes already on fire. I went,

"S'up?"

The Budweiser ref was lost on her. She gushed,

"Guess what?"

"You won the Lotto?"

Seemed to be an Irish response.

"No. Professor de Burgo offered me a position as a research assistant and he'll help me return to college as a mature student."

I felt fingers of ice sneak along my spine. Before I could say something reckless, she said,

"I knew you'd be delighted for me. It means I can talk to you properly about your work."

I wanted to protest,

"Jack is my work."

But went with,

"What about your job?"

She lit up even more.

"Oh, sweetheart, that is so you. Concerned for my welfare."

Uh-huh.

She continued,

"I can still keep my day job and do the research in the evenings."

Halle-fuckin-lujah.

More.

"The professor has great admiration for you."

Yeah . . . right.

Her effusiveness was not catching. I tried for something that wouldn't sound sour, sound lame, I went with,

"I wonder why he chose you?"

Her expression changed and not for the good. She snapped,

"What does that mean?"

This is where a smart guy folds his tent. But no, dumb ass had to push it.

Like this,

"Just seems odd that with all the hundreds of students actually there, I mean, who are like, you know, really students?"

Oh, fuck!

She was on it, repeated, with venom,

"Really students!"

You're in a hole, stop friggin digging. I dug.

"You know what I mean. It's not like you're an obvious Lit type."

Sweet Jesus, did I say that aloud?

She stared at me for a long moment, as if really seeing me, then literally drew back, gathered her things, said,

"Fuck you."

And was gone.

The barman came by, asked,

"Anything else?"

"Something seriously amnesiac."

Jack was listening to a very drunk guy who was in mid-monologue. The diatribe had begun in a vaguely promising manner, with even flashes of a sub-Proust/Joycean flavor, but was deteriorating fast.

Like,

"So, Jack, I'm asking you, there's this guy on *I'm a Celebrity* . . . the fuckin awful jungle reality show. This bollix has got a ten-thousand-euro Rolex and, I kid you not, he's an adult but he cannot read the time."

He stops, astounded by the lunacy and bewildered by the Jameson. Shook his head, continued,

". . . What's with the world, Jack, like we're celebrating the culture of ignorance. That wanker Simon Cowell says the secret to success is being lazy and lucky."

He stared at a fresh pint, a Jay as old outrider, puzzlement on his face, like

"How'd that happen?"

Shrugged, reached for one.

A low rumble came from the man's stomach and an almost rictus crawled down from his hairline. Jack knew that gig. Had borne lonely witness to it his own lonely self, a thousand times over every brand of toilet bowl on the planet. Jack looked around, no one else noticed and certainly no one cared.

He said quietly,

"Incoming."

The man vomited all over the counter. A small volcano of Technicolor gunk. A piece of green testified to the last attempt at food. People were backing away fast, exclaiming,

"Aw, for fuck's sake."

Or

"There goes the neighborhood."

Jack turned to the barman, said,

"Now that's a Kodak moment."

Aine refused to answer my calls. I even fell back on the hackneyed gesture of flowers. They were returned. Sat on my coffee table, slowly dying. My mother had believed if you slip an aspirin into the water, the flowers will last.

Right.

Like my life, they withered. In studying Jack, I had fallen into the most obvious trap for a biographer. I was too close. Worse, in many ways my life was now imitating Jack's. I had alienated my few friends, driven away my girlfriend, and, oh, sweet heaven, not only was I talking like him, I was steadily drinking like him. To some, strolling into a pub, having the barman holler,

"The usual?"

is some lame sign of arrival.

The fuck with that.

See, even the cussing.

A more worrying trait was the anger. Close up I had witnessed Jack's volatile temper. When in doubt, he lashed out. The gauge was permanently set at aggressive.

I found a new simmering rage developing daily. All my brief life, I had been the mellow dude, my mantra,

"Whoa, let it slide, buddy."

I'd discovered a curious phenomenon about living alone.

The utter stillness.

If you don't move, nothing does. The very air seems to be suspended. Then you walk the length of the apartment, it's as if you are part of that atmosphere and it closes behind you. No wonder people crammed their homes with kids, TV, radio, dogs, other people. Noise to break that eerie silence. Jack punctuated it with Jameson. I was beginning to understand a little more of what drove him.

I'd been almost feverish in my compulsion to contact Aine. Had been to her apartment probably a few more times than was prudent. Her roommate finally said,

"Just fuck off."

And, too, I probably sent more texts than was appropriate. Worse, I'd been to her mother's house. Oh, Gawd, wish I hadn't. The woman was polite but adamant, advised,

"Time for you to move on, son."

Still. I thought, if I could see her . . . Hung around the college until a porter finally asked me my business.

I didn't play that well and though he didn't actually lay hands on me, he did say,

"Don't let me catch you here again."

How did this even happen? I was a successful American doctoral candidate with a prestigious scholarship and I was skulking around like a love-torn puppy.

Not cool, dude.

Then the oddest thing. I had been out all day, paying utilities, soaking up the Galway vibe, even spoke to Jimmy Norman, the coolest DJ on Galway radio. The guy had, get this, a cordon bleu, a master's degree in business, a daily show on early morning radio . . . and . . . a pilot's license. The whole new man . . . seriously? And when I had coffee with him, he amazed me with his knowledge of local politics. I felt I was becoming, if not one of the players, at least the guy who knew them. Then, on to the *Galway Advertiser* to meet with Declan Varley, the editor, and Kernan Andrews, the arts/entertainment, go-to guy. All these dudes were young, smart, clued in, and a testament to the whole new generation of Irish who bowed down to freaking nobody. I was pumped, wired on possibilities. To be American in Galway was still to be blessed with remnants of Kennedy afterglow. On the fiftieth anniversary of JFK's death, it was still currency to be a Kennedy. Man, I played that gene card.

Got back to my apartment, buzzing, the endless possibilities, and then . . .

Something off.

Stood in the middle of my living room, sensed the air had been disturbed. A new presence had, oh, so slightly, altered the air. I checked thoroughly. My iPad, TV, all there. The sense of an intruder was almost palpable. I didn't know what to make of it. I also didn't know that by this stage Aine had been dead for two days.

Because nothing was taken, it never occurred to me that

Something . . .

might have been added.

Miscellaneous notes, quotes, chapter headings, descriptions Boru had intended to flesh out his Taylor book

Manic Street Preacher Richard Edwards was crucified by many Hounds of Heaven —
    clinical and manic depression
    anorexia
    alcoholism
    self-mutilation
He walked out of his hotel room in 1995 and was never seen again.

And yet you want to believe that in the place you've come to, where God has allowed you to prosper and for a few generations at least be safe, you honor your religion by doing this. By making something stunningly beautiful:

The Story of the Jews with Simon Schama.

Jack's physical appearance was a testament to the myriad of
    beatings
    muggings
    hammerings
    he'd received by
              hurly
    hammer

baseball bat (s)

shotgun (sawed-off)

He had a distinctive limp and a hearing aid, and two fingers of his right hand had been removed by rusty pliers.

His eyes had the nine-yard stare of long-term convicts doing hard time. Hard time was the mantra of his bedraggled, violent existence.

The years of Jameson, Guinness, and coffin-nail cigarettes had lent to his voice a hoarse, creaky rasp.

The difference between a person who says
"Bring it on"
as opposed to
"Bring it"
is the difference between a person who comes at
you verbally
as opposed to
with a hatchet.
It's very simple.
It's intent.

James A. Emanuel's more than a poet,
more than an ex-pat: a man.
  (Stanley Trybulski on the passing of a great poet,
  as written on Stanley's blog, *Mean Streets*)

Slick lizard rhythms
            cigar smoke
            straight gin
            sky laced with double moons.

Pinned on Jack's wall was a print of Fabritius's *Goldfinch*.
It's a tiny thing.
            Tiny bird
                  Tiny picture
                        Bare wall.
Most telling is that the tiny bird is chained. That this
bird has for centuries represented
Christ on the Cross,
Alone,
Suspended.
The city of Galway was Jack's very own cross.
Jack had been watching Denis Leary's series *Rescue
Me* in what they were now terming a viewing splurge.
Meaning, you have one mega cluster-fuck of the boxed
set back-to-back.
Get this,
Series One through Six in one slam dunk until,
Bleary-eyed,

Dizzy,

Souped

And the wild, crazy world of firefighters seems more real than the wet dreary days of a cold Galway November. Tommy (Denis Leary) could have been Jack,

alcoholic,

screwup,

addict,

violent,

Catholic,

smoker.

Halfway decent shell of a human being. Too, in one way or another, Jack had been putting out fires all his befuddled life.

Starting them, too.

And shards, snippets of the Brooklyn catalog banged around in Jack's head. More real than any lame conversation he'd attempted in any given Galway pub.

"I'm doing you a solid."

Yeah.

Save Jack hadn't, nohow, done anyone "a solid" for a very long time. So, ridding the world of scum like de Burgo might be his very own

White Arrest.

October 28, 2013: Jack heard of the death of Lou Reed at seventy-one on the very day he'd resolved to yet again try a spell of sobriety. He didn't of course confuse sobriety with sanity. The nondrinking patches he'd endured simply seemed to spotlight his areas of madness in stark relief. Back in the day as a Guard, through subterfuge and bribery, he'd landed the security gig for a Reed concert in Dublin. It was a small venue and Lester Bangs's description of Reed as a deformed, depraved midget seemed cruelly apt. It was the high or low of Reed's heroin daze. Dressed in black leather jacket, skintight leather pants, black boots, and the obligatory black shades, he'd mumbled, stuttered, and pretty much failed to deliver a version of "Walk on the Wild Side." He resembled a crushed tarantula devoid of any sting. Helping Reed limp to his dressing room, sweat washing away the white makeup, Jack had ventured.

"Good gig, Mr. Reed."

A mumbled response.

Only later, while he was sinking a Jameson and creamy pint in Doheny & Nesbitt on Baggot Street, did the mutter crystallize.

It was,

"Ya cunt."

Jack smiled, whispered,

"Wild side me arse."

The classic murder victim, if you like,
in today's terminology:
A single, middle-aged man, socially
marginalized with a serious alcohol dependency.
   (Leif G.W. Persson, *He Who Kills the Dragon*.
   Your standard piss-head, basically, was how
   Detective Backstrom described the victim.)

Part II

Jack's Back

Owen Daglish was a guard of the old school.

Rough,

Blunt,

Non-PC,

and one hell of a hurler.

My kind of cop. Unlike me, he hadn't walloped anyone in authority.

Yet.

But it was there, simmering. His superiors knew it, so he was never going to climb the ranks. He didn't arse-kiss, either, so he was doomed to uniform. He and I had some history and most of it was pretty decent. A big man, he was built on spuds, bacon, Guinness, and aggression. Why we got along.

I met him on Shop Street, his day off, and he said,

"Jack, we need to grab a pint."

"Sure, how you fixed this evening?"

He glanced furtively around. Fragile as his job prospects were, it definitely wouldn't help to be seen with me. He grabbed my arm, insisted,

"Now."

Anyone else, he'd have lost the hand from the elbow. I asked,

"I'm presuming something discreet?"

He nodded.

Close to the docks is one of those rare to rarest places. A pub without bouncers and probably without a license. Under-the-radar business is its specialty. That plus serious drinking. No

Wine spritzers,

Bud Lite,

Karaoke.

We got the pints in, grabbed a shaky table in a shaky corner. No word until damage was done to the black. Owen, the creamy top of the Guinness giving him a white mustache, sighed, said,

" 'Tis a bad business."

No one, not even Jimmy Kimmel, can delay a story like the Irish. The preparation is all. *Bad business* could mean a multitude:

The government,

The economy,

Priests,

X Factor,

The weather.

I waited.

He said,

"A young girl found murdered a few days back, part-time student I think."

My radar beeped.

"She was . . . gutted. What's the word? . . . eviscerated."

He looked as if he was going to throw up, rallied, shouted at the bar guy,

"Couple of Jamesons, make them large."

144

He wiped his brow, said,

"I tell you, Jack, like yer ownself, I've seen some ugly shit. You learn to shut off, like the nine-yard stare. You're watching but you're not seeing. Jesus!"

I'm an Irish guy, we don't do the tactile. Keep your friggin hands to yourself. Whoa, yeah, and your emotions, too. Keep those suckers, as they said in *Seinfeld*,

"in the vault."

But I reached over, gently touched his shoulder.

"The last bit, Jack, fuck, the final touch . . ."

It didn't register. He downed the Jay, let that baby weave its wicked magic, shuddered, then,

"A six-inch nail was hammered between her eyes."

I thought,

. . . Nailed!

I spotted an East European guy across the bar. We had business in the past,

Heavy,

Risky

Business.

I indicated a meet with my right hand and he nodded. I said to Owen,

"I need a minute."

In mid-narrative, he was jolted back to where we actually were, protested,

"But there is something else, Jack."

There was always *something else* and never — ever — good.

"One second,"

I said.

In the small smoker's shed at the back, he was waiting, sucking fiercely on one of the cheap Russian cigarettes currently flooding the city. He shook my hand, said,

"Jack, my friend, you need some merchandise?"

Over the years, that had mainly been muscle and dope.

I made the universal sign of my thumb, trigger hammer coming down. He booted the cigarette, took out his mobile, spat some foreign command in a harsh tone, grimaced, clicked off, asked,

"A Ruger, is OK?"

"Sure."

"One box of shells?"

"Perfect."

No money exchanged. That would be later, on delivery.

Got back to Owen. He was literally wringing his hands, went,

"Jesus, times like this, I wish I still smoked. You gave up, didn't you, Jack?"

For an alarming moment I thought he meant it literally, like on life, but focused, shrugged, said,

"Nope, still smoking."

He cracked a smile at that, said — quoted a line from *Charley Varrick*,

"Last of the Independents."

Even Walter Matthau was dead, and recently the great Elmore Leonard. Deferring the final piece of Owen's story, I told him how Leonard's son called around to visit, saw his wife up on the roof clearing the eaves, asked his dad why she was up there. Elmore said,

"Because she can't write books."

Enough with the stalling, I pushed,

"You had something else, Owen?"

Owen said,

"The American kid you were friendly with?"

Jesus, how long was he going to stretch it? I grilled,

"Yeah?"

"They've arrested him for the girl's murder. As the Brits say, 'they've got him bang to rights.'"

I really believed I had lost the capacity to be shocked. The life I'd lived, I could no longer really tell the difference between a shock and a surprise. Like Owen's Brits . . . I was flabbergasted, asked,

"How, I mean . . . ?"

He caught my confusion, cut past it, said bluntly,

"Bloodied underwear was found under his mattress. Sick little fuck."

I finished my Jameson, hoping to blast the bile in my mouth, the acid in my gut, said,

"He didn't do it."

For a moment it seemed as if Owen would punch me on the shoulder, swerved, settled for,

"Come on, Jack, you liked the kid but, let's face it, you obviously had no idea who he was or what he was capable of."

I stared straight at Owen's eyes. Whatever he saw there, he flinched. I said,

"You know history, buddy. I've looked into the faces of

Rapists,
Psychos,
Stone killers,
Priests
and
Bankers.
Trust me, I know when someone is feral."

Owen's eyes got that shadow tint. He wanted another drink, his blood sang for it, he just didn't want it with me. It's always a revelation, a short, intense chat can bury a friendship cold. He knew too we'd come to a standoff but tried to wrap, said,

"I know that, Jack, but there's something else out there now, something new."

I shrugged,

"Evil is never new, simply a different shade."

He put out his hand, we shook, almost meaning it. I headed back to town, went into a hardware store. Bought a pack of six-inch nails. The guy in the store had remarked,

"Some mild weather, huh?"

Indeed.

December 1 and no rain, no real cold weather. We weren't complaining. He asked,

"You know Mike Diviny?"

I didn't. Said,

"Sure."

"He caught forty mackerel in the docks this morning."

He pronounced them in that distinctive, flat-vowel Galway tone,

Mac — ker — el.

One of the reasons I still had a gra for the town. Farther down Shop Street a group of carol singers were seriously massacring "Jingle Bells." A woman with a collection box shoved it in my face, and not politely. I asked,

"Who are you collecting for?"

Figuring I'd gladly help the Philippines Typhoon Fund. She said,

"Girls' basketball team."

I had to take a breath, rein in my disbelief, then,

"You got to be kidding me."

She was up for it, challenged,

"And what do you suggest they do with their leisure time?"

"Would fishing be out of the question?"

The Ruger was delivered that evening. I paid over the odds; helps the discretion. I was sitting at the table, cleaning the gun as Jimmy Norman's show played on Galway Bay FM. A song rooted me to the chair,

"Mary"
          by Patty Griffin.

My memory kicked in, sometimes supplying arcane and, in truth, useless information. She'd been married briefly to Robert Plant. The lyrics of the song touched me in all the broken places. Heaving the gun amid a mess of bullets, I stood, poured a liberal Jay, toasted Patty, said,

"Your voice is the perfect bridge between Emmylou Harris and Nancy Griffiths."

I tried to get my head around the notion of Boru being a killer. Wouldn't fly. I'd spent enough time with the kid to get his measure. Then a thought hit. I grabbed my mobile, got Owen, said,

"I'm sorry to be bothering you so soon."

"That's OK, Jack. I enjoyed the pints, we should do it more often."

That hovered for a moment but we knew it was never going to happen. I asked,

"The murdered girl, you said she was a part-time student?"

"Yeah."

"Literature, by any chance?"

"Yes. In fact I heard the professor told the investigating officers that Kennedy had been stalking the girl. A college security guard even remembered moving him along."

Fuck, this wasn't good.

He said,

"Leave it alone, Jack. It's cut-and-dried."

I had one last question,

"Who is in charge of the case?"

"A hotshot named Raylan. A man going places, they say."

I didn't know him, said,

"I don't know him."

"You might know his assistant?"

"Yeah?"

"A certain Sergeant Ridge."

★　★　★

Over many turbulent years I have returned to my variety of apartments/flats to find

Ransacking,

Burglary,

Fires,

but never a . . .

Goth.

Sitting on my sofa, apparently at ease, was a young woman in full Goth regalia. The white makeup, black mascara, spiked black hair, and, of course, all-black gear. I said what you'd expect me to say,

"What the fuck?"

She'd helped herself to the Jameson, raised it, said,

"Slainte."

Her utter composure suggested she was one cool lady or on heavy medication. I stayed by the door, asked,

"You want to tell me what's going on?"

"I'm Emerald, like the isle, I suppose, but mostly I prefer Em, less formal."

I said,

"Before I sling you out, you want to tell me why you're here, stealing my booze?"

She stood up, I tensed. A moment, then she said,

"Relax, if I was going to hurt you, would I have sat waiting?"

"Been known to go down exactly like that."

For this I got a brilliant smile, sheer fucking radiance. It warmed something deep in my core that had been dead a long time. Whatever else, I felt she wasn't a threat, leastways not a physical one. She was small but

151

moved with that grace given only to dancers and felines. She said,

"See, you're lightening up already. OK if I call you Jack?"

Before I could answer, she continued,

"Need to alert you, hombre, that I have a form of accent Tourette's. Means I flip from down-home through posh to ni-gg-ah . . ."

She stretched out the final word provocatively. Almost but not quite wetting her lips. She was a piece of work. I tried again,

"Before I knock your multiethnic arse out, you want to give me a hint as to what this is?"

She mimed a gunslinger stance, said,

"It's all about the love, Pilgrim . . . well, no . . . revenge, actually, and that gig is cold, dude."

Jesus!

I went and poured myself a drink, a large one, didn't offer her. She had more than enough of whatever it was drove her batmobile. Was she finished?

Was she fucked.

More.

"So, Jacques, it's all about the endgame and I'm your wingman.

"You wanna know who're we're taking D

O

W

N?"

She pronounced it thus, dropping in register to the last syllable. I said,

"Maybe before the new year, you'll actually tell me?"

152

She threw open her arms in a grand salute, exclaimed,

"El Jefe, the professor, Señor de Burgo, his own badass self."

Got my attention.

As she headed for the door, she stopped, listened, said,

"That wind they've been threatening is finally gathering force."

As to whether this was a metaphor or a weather forecast, who knew? She gave another blast of the wattage smile, said,

"We'll go biblical on the prof's ass, right?"

She looked up at the sky, said,

"Goth in the wind."

The death of Nelson Mandela met with a profound sadness not seen since the death of John F. Kennedy. Alas, the cash vultures were already swooping. Mandela's famous handprint being sold for upwards of twenty thousand euros. It made you want to seriously vomit.

The week before, the incredibly affable, apparently full-blessed Paul Walker, only forty, star of the hugely successful movie franchise *Fast & Furious*, was killed instantly when the Porsche he was a passenger in was wrapped around a tree.

Some weeks it seemed only funerals marked the successive days.

December 12: the feast day of Our Lady of Guadalupe.

The Health Department, in one week, finally admitted liability in three separate cases of babies being neglected by the very medics charged with their care. All three of the little mites, as a result, had:

Massive brain damage,

Cerebral palsy,

Total paralysis.

And a very basic lack of oxygen for a few vital moments had occurred. The HSE took twelve years to admit liability in Case 1, and seven and five years in the other two cases.

The families were utterly exhausted and destroyed but they fought all those years for the most basic human right.

An apology.

The minister for health, fat-jowled and combative, muttered platitudes like,

>Regret
>and
>Investigation.

Dare one curse —

>Don't hold your breath.

All the major charities were exposed as paying their top executives "top-ups" in the hundreds of thousands and they even sneered,

"If you pay peanuts, you get monkeys."

And still they ran long, harrowing advertisements of dying black children with Eva Cassidy singing in the background. Shaming, bullying, and cajoling a bankrupt people into donating what few euros they retained. If the people hated any song, they now hated "Fields of Gold."

Em had agreed to actually tell me who/what she was, if
I got wasted with her.
Her words.
Meaning, go on the piss. Twist my arm.

She insisted we go to the G Hotel. Already noted for its theme rooms, as in: you wanted peace, you opted for the purple room. Em said,

"Guy in the bar there shakes one mean, multifucking cocktail."

I said,

"I don't do fancy."

She got the look, she asked,

"You want the gen on me or not?"

"Guess I could go for a frozen margarita."

She laughed, said,

"Dress to impress, slick."

Been a time since I hit the charity shops. With the recession, the new scandal about top executives of the leading charities on massive salaries, the people on the ground, the actual working staff, were bearing the brunt at the Vincent de Paul shop. Rita greeted me,

"Jack, we thought you'd brought your business to T.J. Maxx."

And swear to God, she gave that Galway hug:

Real,

Warm,

Felt.

And fitted me out with a dark suit that hung a little loose but I can do loose. A Van Heusen shirt and brand new Dr. Martens. The cost —

fifteen euros.

I kid you fucking not.

Heading for the G in my splendor, I shucked into my Garda all-weather coat and was, if not hot to trot, at least ready to limp with attitude.

We were sitting, not close but not distant. From left field she just launched.

"My old man sends me hefty checks for the guilt."

Uh-oh.

"What guilt?"

"For diddling me in every orifice until I was sixteen."

Then she swiveled in her seat, exclaimed,

"Over there, I saw Iain Glen. Be still my heart. He's got that intense brooding gig going."

Then switched again, said,

"Think of me as a cocktail. You take,

Carol O'Connell's Mallory

A note of Sara Gran's Claire DeWitt

A sprinkle of angel dust

Shake that mojo

    And

     Out

     Pops

      Me fein (me!)."

Before I could comment she added,

"You only need to know I'm less Sylvia Plath and more Anne Sexton."

I said,

"Or you could just be full of shite."

We were on our second margaritas and those suckers were sliding down bad and easy. Em took out an e-cig, the green light glowing against the tequila sheen in her eyes. She said,

"I descended into a complete full madness and if you can know and accept that, you can function on a whole other level."

I watched her exhale the nicotine-based water vapor and felt a powerful urge to smoke. A kick-in-the-gut, honest-to-God, unfiltered Lucky Strike. Em continued,

"Some people, before bed, they layout the next day's clothes. Me, I layout a slew of personalities, then, come morning I wake, pop an upper, chase it with a double espresso, and see who I'm going to be that day."

I asked,

"Isn't that tiresome?"

Now, she was coming to it, asked,

"Jack . . ."

Pause.

"Don't you ever want to be somebody else, even for a little while?"

"I'd settle for being some*where* else, even for a little while."

I could feel the tequila, settling then whispering, so I let it talk, said,

"Truth is, I only ever wish to be a fictional character."

She was delighted, asked,

"Oh, do tell, and please . . . sweet Jesus, don't be predictable and do a James Bond shite song . . . let it be colorful!"

I said,

"Raylan Givens, as written by Elmore Leonard. Gets to wear a cool hat and not look like an eejit, has a side that is pure mellow. He's a U.S. marshal."

158

She was disappointed or maybe the booze was on its rota of up/down swings, she said,

"You like him because of the hat?"

"No, because he legally shoots people."

I didn't come to . . . *wake* would be too mild a word, to find myself naked in bed. The events of the night went blank after I'd sat on the sofa with Em.

I staggered out of bed, expecting the thundering hangover tequila guarantees, but no . . . and I certainly shouldn't have slept as soundly as I did. The norm would be the porcelain prayer, i.e., early in the morning (very early) puking my guts over the toilet bowl, on my knees, sweating like be-Jaysus. But no.

Apart from light-headedness, not unpleasant, I appeared to be fine. Fuck, even wanted coffee and a smoke. Pulling on a Galway United long sweatshirt, I went to the front room. A neatly wrapped package on the table with a note.

Lover,
    I slipped you a Mickey Finn lest you
    attempted to slip me some Irish. I was up
    early, fucked with you a little (kidding),
    went out and brought you a present . . . for
    the Raylan in all of us. Catch you nine
    sharp tomorrow. We're heading for
    Portlaoise to visit your young felon. Dress
    for jail!
    Meantime, I brewed fresh coffee so there
    should still be some kick in it . . . like your
    old self really.

Tootle-Pip,
The
Emerald

I poured the coffee, still hot and indeed with a punch and then opened the package.

A perfect cowboy hat, with the snap brim.

You had to love her!

Next morning, I was outside the apartment, no idea what to expect. A yellow VW Beetle pulled up. A very beat-up one. The window rolled down, Em, behind the wheel, said,

"Pickup for a Mr. Taylor?"

She wasn't wearing a chauffeur's hat but her voice had the vibe. She was dressed in lawyer mode again. This time a prim white suit, blue-striped and expensive, hair tied back, sensible shoes.

I got in and she eased into traffic, hit the stereo, and music surrounded us.

I asked,

"A yellow bug . . . really?"

She was trying to identify the song, said,

"I know this? Why? Arcade fire?"

I asked,

"Ever hear of Ted Bundy?"

As we reached the outskirts of the city she reached down, then handed me an iPad.

"Some light reading for the trip."

She said,

"*Taylor* —

Made.

"It's Boru's first draft of his book on you."

"Jesus, how'd you get that?"
She was turning at the traffic circle, said,
"Young man in charge of the Evidence Room."
"Yeah?"
"He has a Britney thing. I donned the outfit from her first video, the school gym? The wet dream of middle-aged guys everywhere."
Skeptical.
"And what, he just gave it to you?"
She fumbled for a flask of coffee, said,
"I gave him a blow job."
Jesus!
I poured the coffee, settled back to read, a way in, thought,
"Holy fuck!"
She asked,
"How you liking it so far, Mr. Johnson?"
"Christ, everybody seems to hate me."
She shrugged, said,
"Now you know how Sting feels."
She asked,
"So where's your manners, bud?"
"Excuse me?"
"You don't feel a wee mite of gratitude for the U.S. marshal hat?"
I let lots of hard leak over my tone, said,
"Rohipnol? Fucking date rape . . . you really want to go there, to revisit the source of the . . . misdemeanor?"
She laughed, mock-shuddered, said,
"Oh . . . scary . . . I think I'm a little turned on."

No real answer to that involves any sanity. I noticed a small logo on the dashboard, read:

Go gangsta,

Go ghetto.

How non-Irish do you get? I asked,

"Might I inquire who you'll be today?"

She used a dashboard lighter to fire up. I kid you not, a fuckin spiff, inhaled deep, said,

"Hope the fuck I don't get the munchies."

Offered me the joint, I said,

"One dope per car seems sufficient."

She snorted, then,

"To answer your previous, in light of this . . ." waved the joint,

". . . I was thinking, Nancy Botwin, you know, from *Weeds*?"

Terse, I snapped,

"I know who she is, Mary-Louise Parker."

She said,

"Jesus, got you already."

Mercifully, we were approaching Portlaoise. She stopped the car suddenly, looked right at me, asked,

"Right now, this moment, what would you most like to be doing?"

"Not sitting here in a yellow bug, not a spit from prison with . . . Sybil."

Her eyes were serious, no dancing lunacy, she said,

"I'm serious, tell me."

"Well, in my apartment, sipping fifty-year-old whiskey from the oak, watching Borgen with maybe the collected short stories of Amy Hempel as backup."

162

I thought I saw a wetness touch her eyes, then she was back to biz, grabbing a battered briefcase, fixing her hair, said,

"That's probably the saddest thing I ever heard."

Portlaoise Prison is Ireland's only high-security prison. Beside it is Midland Prison, a newer medium-security unit.

Built in 1830, it is notorious for the number of Provos there. Now it houses Ireland's most dangerous criminals,

Drug gangs,

Killers,

Rapists.

Irish Republican prisoners are on the old E-Block.

Irish Defense Forces are used as Guards. An exclusion zone operates over the entire complex,

Assault rifles,

Antiaircraft guns.

Notable inmates: Angelo Fusco

Martin Ferris

Dessie O'Hare

John Gilligan

Paul Magee

In 2007, John Daly, an inmate, phoned the radio show *Live Line*. His call resulted in Guards seizing fifteen hundred items of contraband:

Mobile phones

Plasma TVs

and incredibly, a budgie, smuggled in by a visitor concealing it in his buttocks! Whole new meaning to "a bird in the hand" or indeed "doing bird." Daly had to be transferred owing to the death threats from the inmates.

Released in 2007, he was celebrating with a night out and was murdered.

The Caged Bird Sang No More.

I asked,

"Who are we supposed to be to gain entrance?"

She was all manic energy now, said,

"I'm the lawyer of note and you are the beloved, elderly Irish uncle."

"Hey, enough with the elderly."

She nearly smiled, said,

"Least you won't have to work hard to get into character."

The Guards gave us the full security gig, eye-fucking as they did. Eventually, we were led into a small room, told No. 2035789 would be along shortly. Em, who for reasons best known to herself had adopted a haughty Brit accent, snapped,

"He does have a name."

The Guard, delighted he had riled her, said,

"Not in here."

Pause.

"Ma'am."

The tone was,

Bitch!

We sat on hard metal chairs, a beat-up table before us. Someone had gouged into the top:

Kilroy was here

. . . didn't last

Deep.
She said,
"You never asked what my ideal moment would be."
As the door opened, I said,
"Like I give a shit."

"Let he who has not been stoned
cast the first sin."

A warden, built like a brick shithouse, led Boru into the room. He was dressed in faded denims, way too large. He looked like a twelve-year-old. The warden pushed him to a chair, facing us, then moved back to stand, arms folded, against the wall. A heavy link chain circled the guy's belt, clanked as he moved. It was the sound of punishment. Boru never looked up, his head down like a penitent's.

Em barked at the warden in a Maggie Thatcher "*Don't fuck with me*" tone.

"Some privacy please."

Reluctantly, slowly, he withdrew. I said,

"Boru, hey buddy, it's Jack."

He raised his head as if it hurt. A dark bruise ran from his right eye all down to his jaw. It looked swollen. I didn't ask.

"How are you?"

How he was, was badly fucked. I said,

"This is Em, she's going to get you out."

Yeah, right.

Boru said, his mouth revealing a bloody gap where his fine American front teeth had been,

"I want to go home."

It reminded me of Thomas Wolfe's *You Can't Go Home Again*.

I didn't share this literary gem. Em asked,

"Besides the underwear they found, has your lawyer said the prosecutors have anything else?"

He looked at her, his eyes off-kilter, then,

"I didn't take her . . . intimate things."

Em slammed the table hard with the palm of her hand, startling Boru and me. She snapped,

"Get with the program, kid . . . man up for Chrissake."

It focused him, he tried,

"Don't be mean to me."

Unrelenting, she pushed,

"We're all you've got. Now I want to know if the bloody knickers are all they've got."

He stammered,

"The st . . . stalking, they say . . . I did that."

She waved it off.

"Overzealous admiration, no biggie."

She stood up, said,

"I think we're done here."

Boru was amazed, pleaded,

"Can't you stay a bit?"

She was already gathering her things, said,

"No offense, kiddo, but you're hardly riveting company."

He turned to me, asked,

"Jack, will I get out?"

He might get out but, judging by his appearance, he wasn't ever coming back.

170

In the movies, this is where the good guy reassures,

"Stay strong, we'll get you out."

And other such shite.

I said,

"Keep your head down."

Em added,

"But try not to give head."

She pounded the door, shouted,

"Yo, Cruickshank, we're done."

I didn't give Boru a comforting pat on the shoulder. He'd been touched enough.

Back in the car, I asked,

"You got a cig?"

She did.

We fired up, then she blew rubber as we got the hell out of there. Ten minutes in, she said,

"Saga Norén, in case you were wondering."

The fuck was she on about? I asked,

"What?"

"Who I'd like to be. The icy, semi-autistic cop in *The Bridge*." I said,

"You're not even blond — well, least not today."

She shot past a BMW like a dervish, said,

"Yeah, but I got the bitch part down cold."

We stopped in Oranmore for a drink. She ordered a toasted sandwich, like this,

"Highly grilled cheddar,

hint of mayo,

rye bread."

The guy taking the order simply slapped a prewrapped job in the microwave, zapped it.

I took a Jameson.

No ice.

"Your treat," she said, looking at the expensive bill.

I didn't argue. Then she asked,

"Have you plans for Christmas Day?"

"Cold turkey."

She was interested, asked,

"You're giving up . . . what?"

"Nothing. I'll eat my turkey cold with a pack of Lone Star longnecks and watch *Breaking Bad*'s spin-off series on Netflix."

She had no answer to that, so I asked,

"And you?"

Thinking, "Who'll you be that day?"

No hesitation,

"I'm going to Prague with my boyfriend."

Jesus, come on, did I feel a pang of . . . fuckin . . . jealousy?

I managed,

"What's he do?"

"He's a felon . . . and a poet. A poetic felon, you might say."

I went with,

"Sounds like a blast."

I paid. We were heading for the car, she said,

"He's hung like a stallion."

Indeed.

Em's lunacy, Boru's fucked state, the shadow of the prison, led me to need some time alone but not on my own, if you catch my drift. To be among people but not part of them. Christmas eve, the city is on the piss so a quiet pub is a scarcity. Paddy Fahy's in Bohermore is a haven. It has a certain dress code — no assholes allowed.

I sat at the counter. The owner, Paddy, is blessed with the gift of silence. Five people in total made up the clientele. I was working on my second expertly pulled pint, a large Jameson holding point. A man two stools away was working on his own solitude. I had the *Irish Independent* books section open before me. The year's top sellers looked like this:

(1) *Padre Pio*
(2) *The GAA: A People's History*
(3) *Gone Girl*
(4) *One Direction*
(5) *Niall Horan: The Unauthorized Biography*
(6) *X-Factor Encyclopaedia*
(7) *Alex Ferguson: My Autobiography*.

I sighed. The guy two stools down caught it, raised his pint, nodded. Now I remembered him. When I had a drink with Boru in Jury's, I'd told him about the man who odd times drank there.

Always alone.

He'd done some hard time in a South American jail. So rumor said. He certainly had the lost eyes to give it credence. I'd heard too he had a minor rap going as a crime writer.

On impulse, I asked,

"Buy you a pint?"

No answer.

Pushed,

"It being the season and all that good shite."

Cracked the remotest smile, then,

"Yeah, what the hell."

And he moved to stand next to me. I signaled Paddy, who reached for the Jameson. The man's movements were slow and calculated as if energy was vital and spared. He raised his glass, said,

"Slainte amach."

His voice was neutral, not toneless but more used to silence. He nodded at the books page, said,

"Guy there, last week, he tore my book to shreds."

I took a hefty swipe of my own Jay, asked,

"That bother you?"

He gave a short laugh, said,

"They try to wipe you off the floor of a cell containing thirty desperate inmates, what do you think?"

What did I think?

The booze or the craziness of the past year made me pushy or thoughtless. I asked,

"How does a person . . . you know, handle that, I mean, after, when you're out?"

He studied the top shelf, scanning the variety of lethal spirits, then,

"You get a shitty bed-sit in Brixton, then you get an old-fashioned revolver, with the spin chamber. Every Wednesday, seven in the evening, you sit and spin that sucker."

Christ!

Reckless now, I asked,

"Why Wednesday?"

He put twenty euros on the counter, turned up his coat collar, said,

"Never liked midweek much."

He nodded to Paddy, indicating a drink for me. I put out my hand, said,

"I'm Jack Taylor."

He gave me a long hard look, not threatening, just resolute, said,

"Oh, I know who you are."

And he was gone.

Professor de Burgo had his feet up on his desk, the lion in the lair. Books scattered everywhere, potpourri overriding the smell of pot. De Burgo was on his third Americano, anticipating the young female undergraduate due in . . .

He extracted his gold pocket watch from his tartan waistcoat, a theatrical, well-rehearsed gesture. Even

175

alone, he repeated the rituals necessary to re-inform the whole

"old-fashioned, John Cheever-type
professor of English literature."

She was due in twenty minutes. In twenty days she'd be history. He suppressed a giggle at his own wit, popped half a Valium, get the mellow gig cooking. Began to sift through his in-box. A small padded envelope called. He sliced it open with a heavy silver Moroccan letter opener and the color drained from his sunlamped face.

A six-inch nail —
The letters — ed.

Nailed!

Badly shaken, de Burgo pulled another envelope from the pile. A bright pink envelope and . . . hold a mo —

Perfumed!

Fuck, yes, actually scented! He chuckled (this is a parched sound as he'd been told it made him *lovable*).

Figuring it to be from one of the many moonfaced cunts who adored his lectures, he opened it with a flourish and

out
tumbled
tiny white and black paper figures wearing? Mortar-boards. A note on lilac paper read,

This is Sancta Muerta,
the Death Curse . . . on you.
The figures amount to the number

of days until you burn in hell.
Xxxxxxxxx
Kalinda
P.S. Kalinda is PI/vengeance chick from
the series *The Good Wife*.

Feverishly, he counted the fragile figures.
Six!
He crumpled them in a rage-fueled dread. Reached
into his desk, took out a bottle of Grey Goose, lashed
into it.
A knock on the door, then a pretty girl's head peered
around the door, asked,
"Am I on time, professor?"
He flung a copy of the collected Blake at her,
shouted,
"Get the fuck!"

Cambridge's Hampers, a Galway Christmas tradition.
Not cheap, but oh, so fabulous. Chockablock with
every goody you could yearn for. One was delivered to
my apartment on Christmas eve.
A note:

Knock yourself out Jack.
Your very own dark
Emerald
Xxxxxxx

What I remember of Christmas Day is the wild storms,
not only in my head but in the weather. A falling tree

177

killed a twenty-three-year-old who'd just passed her driving test. It came right through the windscreen.

The racing ace Schumacher was preparing his ski gear for a week of exhilaration.

I watched the original BBC series of *Tinker, Tailor, Soldier, Spy*. Alec Guinness was, as always, riveting. I spaced the day between

Snacks of cold turkey

Xanax, 2.5 mg

Single hot whiskeys

              no cloves.

The mobile rang once.

Ridge.

A flood of relief that she was prepared to wish me,

"Nollaig Sona Duit" (Happy December).

She wasn't.

Lashed,

"Taylor, you want to explain to me who that mad bitch was?"

My bile in check, I said gently,

"Need a bit more to go on. I know quite a few bitches, but mad? That's relative."

Heard her angry rasp in a deep breath, then,

"Don't play the cute hoor, the supposed lawyer who showed up at our last meet."

I had a choice. It being the season of goodwill, would I goodwill it?

No.

Went for annoyance.

"Gotta plead the Fifth."

A beat, then,

"Don't suppose she knows anything about the disappearance of the underwear, vital to the Boru Kennedy case?"

My heart soared.

"Good fuck, really? So you've no case now."

"Fuck you, Taylor."

Slammed the phone down.

In the early hours of Christmas morning, Boru had used a sheet to hang himself.

The case was truly CLOSED.

Late Christmas night, my mind was crawling with snakes. Desperate to distract, I had a mini Ben Wheatley fest.

Down Terrace

Kill List

Sightseers — with the line after the main character beats a guy to death and says,

"Not a human, a *Daily Mail* reader."

Doesn't come any darker or more blackly humorous. My life in disjointed glances really. Saint Stephen's morning, my hangover was what you'd expect.

Rough.

The doorbell rang.

A group of disheveled singers, I kid thee fucking not.

Either the Wren (and do they still continue this tradition?) or the remnants of a soused hen party. I gave them a few notes on condition they stopped singing!

Two kick-ass coffees,

Solpadine,

Xanax,

And, God help me, one sick cigarette. My mind began to twist.

I phoned Ridge.

She answered with a terse,

"Taylor?"

"You know Boru Kennedy was innocent on Christmas eve?"

Sigh.

"Yes."

"Did you tell him or did his lawyer?"

"Not my job, Taylor."

"You cunt."

Stunned gasp,

"What did you call me?"

"He spent Christmas eve not knowing he was clear. Terrorized, terrified . . . what was he anticipating, Christmas dinner? That some big bastard would take off him. This was a kid who'd spent every Christmas safe, warm, and with a family!"

She spat her words,

"Don't . . . you . . . dare put this on me, Taylor."

"You got your wish, sergeant. You've become a real Guard."

"How dare you."

"Have a nice New Year, see the sheets you helped strangle that poor, lost kid in a dark cell."

I slammed down the phone.

Days blundered through the post-Christmas gloom. Sales, despite the recession, had people sleeping outside Brown Thomas for thirty-six hours to secure

180

Gucci handbags!

The homeless just slept outside anywhere and for longer. Covered in piss, despair, and degradation.

Recession my arse, as a woman got lead story on RTE six o'clock news for buying a Stella McCartney dress for only fifteen hundred euros!

The New Year galloped toward us. Em hadn't returned nor phoned. Maybe she'd fucked off permanently.

Did I care?

Not a whole bunch.

I was too broken, heartsick over the needless waste of Boru's suicide. Was I to blame? I was certainly in the mix. A horrible irony wasn't lost on me that the coveted number one song was by a prison guard.

Hang your guilt on that.

Ken Dodd on the first
sign of aging —
"When you wake up and find you've a bald-headed
son."

January 3, 2013.
  My birthday.
  Fuck
        and
  Fuck
        Again.
I got over thirty cards. Yeah, right!
I dragged my aging body to the shower, avoided the mirror, not a mix. I was growing a beard. At that stage of weary wino, not to mention leery. I had a serious adrenalized coffee and an extra Xanax for the day that was in it.
  My head was scrambled for a blitz night of TV.
  A highly anticipated return of Benedict Cumberbatch as Sherlock Holmes on BBC. Then, mid-Jameson, I switched to Sky Living to catch Jonny Lee Miller as Sherlock. After midnight, on cable, I stumbled across . . . you guessed it . . . Sherlock with Robert Downey Jr. in the role. I fell into bed with Basil Rathbone striding through my dreams uttering,
            "I'm the real deal."
  Come morning,
  I dressed like a winner.

Sort of.

Old Garda sweatshirt under a weird fish comfortable wool shirt. Black 500s over Dr. Martens. Shucked into my all-weather item 1834, looked out the window, said,

"Bring it on."

Guilt-free for once to hit Garavan's at opening time. Sean the barman said,

"Blian Nua go maith."

Indeed.

Two drinks in, a guy took the stool beside me. I tried for his name,

"Tom?"

He nodded, ordered a large Paddy, no ice. Got my vote.

I knew his backstory. A rough one. His son had been killed by a nineteen-year-old drunk driver. Worse, if possible, the guy walked, on a technicality. Tom then had the horror of running into this pup fairly regularly. Galway is still a village in the worst way.

The punk, far from repentant, would smirk, even once flashing a thumbs-up.

Until . . .

Six months before, the punk, drunk, got behind the wheel of his brand-new Audi. Present from Daddy for his twenty-first. A figure in the backseat shoved a single long shaft of steel into the base of his skull, right to the dumb fuck's brain. Tom had a solid alibi.

He ordered a second drink, offered me one.

My birthday!

So I said,

"Yeah, thank you."

We clinked glasses, I said,

"You doing OK?"

He held his drink up to the light, as if it might reveal some truth. Then he smiled, said,

"The past six months, I've been fucking great."

Amen.

Sean, a voracious reader, watched Tom leave, then put a book on the counter. It was upside down but I could read the author's name,

Sara Gran.

Sean freshened my pint, said.

"I read an author during Christmas and you know, the critics crap him off because they say . . ."

Pause

". . . Get this. He uses too many cultural references, pop music, crime writers in his books. Now, see, you know what I think of them? I might hazard . . . not complimentary?"

Big grin, then,

"Yeah, bollix to them. Because for me, it grounds the story in stuff I know, that I can relate to. One fuck said he was for people who don't read. How fucking insulting is that to readers?"

The pint was good. I sank a quarter, said,

"Thing is, Sean, critics are God's excuse for why shite happens."

Sean was shouted at by a small elderly woman who demanded,

"A big dry sherry."

As he turned to go, he said,

"Hey, guess whose birthday is today."
I tried for a humble grin, asked,
"Who?"
"Schumacher."
Michael Schumacher was in a medically induced coma.

I reflected bitterly that in one form or another, I had been inducing a coma over my whole bedraggled life.

Back at my apartment I found Johnny Duhan had sent me a copy of his album
                    Winter.
The very first track might have been written by my own heart,
                    "Charity of Pain."
I muttered,
"God bless your genius soul, Johnny."
Marc Roberts and Jimmy Norman, over the past week, had been giving extensive airplay to "The Beacon."
Serendipity?
I dunno, but later in the week, my favorite band, the Saw Doctors, were due in the Roisin Dubh.
Music, music everywhere and not a hand to hold.
Och, ochon (woe is rife).

"You can run with the big dogs
or sit on the porch and bark."
(Wallace Arnold)

January 5: Horrendous gales and storms continued to lash the country.

In Salthill, the sea roared over the promenade to submerge the Toft car park.

It was surreal to see the cars floating in more than six feet of water. Homes, hospitals were without power. That evening, I risked a walk to see the damage. Headed for the cathedral. A vague notion that I might light some candles for all my dead . . . a long list.

The church was closed. Priests lining up for sales, no doubt. I was about to turn into Nun's Island when something caught my eye. A figure, outlined against the heavy church door, was kicking something repeatedly.

A desperate penitent?

I have never been troubled with minding my own business. I headed over, realizing it was a guy in his twenties kicking the be-Jaysus out of a tiny pup.

I shouted,

"Hey, shithead, you want to stop doing that."

He turned, well turned-out in a North Face heavy parka, matching combat pants, and thick Gore-Tex boots. His face was tanned, well nourished. Who the fuck has a tan in Galway in January?

He seemed delighted to see me.

You believe it?

Flashed brilliant white teeth that testified to seriously expensive dentistry. This kid came from money. He reached into his jacket, produced a large knife; it glinted off the heavy brass door handles. He said in that quasi surfer dude accent the youngsters (the stupid ones) have adopted,

"You want a piece of me?"

He actually ran it as *wanna*. Whatever movie was running in his head, it had a definite x-cert. The pup, whimpering, tried to huddle more into the wall under the holy water font. The poor thing looked like a refugee from Bowie's album *Space Oddity*, or maybe more *Diamond Dogs*.

I said,

"Why don't you come down here and we'll see what we can do with the knife?"

He literally leaped the five steps and I sidestepped, putting all of a right fist into his gut. I kicked him in the head as he crumpled. Then I caught him by the scruff of the neck, pulled him back up to the holy water font, pushed his head in it, said,

"Count your blessings."

I counted to ten, pulled him out, reached in his jacket, found a fat wallet. Took that. I leaned down, gathered up the tiny bundle of terrorized pup, moved him into the warmth of my jacket. The guy was groaning, his eyes coming back into focus, and, swear to God, somehow he managed a malevolent smile, muttered,

192

"Your ass is grass, dude."

With the heel of my Dr. Martens, I destroyed that fabulous dental art. I turned to go and, in fair imitation of his accent, said,

"Doggone!"

I called the pup . . . what else . . .

"Ziggy."

Over the next few days I spent a small fortune on vet treatment. I'd been feeding him, sparingly, from the finger of a rubber glove, blend of

Sugar

Warm milk

Jameson.

He was the quietest pup the vet ever encountered.

I said,

"He has a lot to be quiet about."

He fitted in the palm of my hand, melting brown eyes and snow-white paws. He was, the vet said,

"A cross between a terrier and a pug."

"A mongrel?"

I said.

The vet nodded.

"Like myself,"

I ventured.

He didn't disagree.

The psycho's wallet yielded a driver's licence in the name of Declan Smyth. Credit cards (gold) and other data revealed him to be nineteen, a student of engineering at NUIG.

A member of Galway's foremost lap dancing club. (We had a lap dancing club?).

Where?

There was a nice tidy package of coke, some "E" tabs, and close to six hundred in notes. Paid for the vet.

Google threw up that Dec lived at home in Taylor's Hill with his father, a pediatrician of note; and his mother, a runner-up in the Rose of Tralee. The family had no pets.

Keith Finnegan was reading the news. I heard this:

"A young student from a prominent family was savagely beaten in a mugging outside Galway Cathedral as he attempted to attend midnight Mass."

Unless they were now offering Black Masses, the Guards had failed to notice the locked doors.

To ensure Ziggy's warmth and sense of belonging, I placed him in a Galway United sweatshirt beside my pillow at night.

I woke in the morning to find him snuggled sound asleep on my chest.

He was adapting.

It was like a scene from an
Armageddon movie. Large boulders
were thrown over the wall onto the
car park by the sea.

(Comment on the storm by
Joe Garrity,
manager of Sea World
in County Clare)

A card from Arizona read:

Jack-o,
    I went to the Poisoned Pen Bookshop.
Met a hot guy named Patrick Milliken and
Heard Jim Sallis read. That dude rocks.
Back soon.
                Xxxxxxxxxxxxx
                Your greenish Em

Ziggy was improving rapidly, already knew where the treats were. Chewed on every available table, chair, bed leg. It was a given he would be lying next to my pillow. That was oddly endearing.

I kept up a nigh daily posting of nails to de Burgo. Oiled and cleaned the Ruger daily. Visualizing putting two rounds in the fucker's balls.

The storms continued to lash holy hell out of the west coast. I so wanted to bring the pup to run on the Salthill beach but the ferocity of the Atlantic on Galway Bay would be too much.

He'd already had a lash of Galway ferocity.

The Guards were now saying they had an eyewitness to the mugging of the young man at Galway Cathedral.

Were they blowing smoke? I sure hoped to fuck they were.

Noon that Thursday, I opened the door to . . . Em. The pup peeping from behind my legs. She was dressed . . . Parisian chic? Pale leather coat, black polo, and — surely not — leather pants over black boots. Her hair was now in that elfin cute brown style like the poster of *Amélie*, the French movie. She greeted me,

"Bon soir mon fils et le petit chien."

She had a rugged worn gladstone bag which she handed to me, said,

"Snap to it, Jeeves."

Despite the nonsense, I was glad to see her. Nearly . . . nearly hugged her.

She breezed in and, with one fluid gesture, scooped up the pup, said,

"Vas bon, mon chéri."

Plunked herself on the couch, the pup already snug in her arms, said,

"So, let's make with the beverages, Jacques."

I built some fine hot toddies, even lit a cig, and as I handed it to her, a loud thump rattled the door. I muttered,

". . . the fuck?"

Opened it to Ridge and a new face to me, in a crisp new uniform. He looked about twelve but a mean little twelve. Viciousness already marking his eyes. She ordered,

"Jack Taylor, I need to interview you in relation to a very serious assault."

I swept my arms wide, said,

"Do come in."

She stopped on seeing Em, the recruit nearly colliding with her back. She said,

"The ubiquitous Em?"

Ridge always had a tell. I had tried. I had tried to clue her on it, comparing it to a royal flush. But she brushed it off as

"Drink shite talk."

Eyeing the dog, she opened with,

"Mr. Taylor, we have a witness who describes a man resembling you as being the assailant in a vicious mugging."

Em, slowly lighting a slim cigarette with a gold lighter, asked,

"The time and date, sergeant?"

Ridge glared at her, looked at the travel bag, played the queen, asked,

"Been traveling?"

"I was in Korea but that was some time ago, the bag is dirty laundry. Feel free to root about in it. I sense that's your forte."

Ridge, red color climbing up her cheeks, reined in, gave the time and day.

The recruit, whose name I learned was Costello, glared at me. I said,

"Not sure if . . ."

I glanced at the pup,

"You have a dog in this fight, son?"

The "son," rattled, looked to Ridge, who ignored him. Em said,

"Jack and I were . . . what's the buzz term? . . . *en flagrant* the evening in question."

Ridge went for her king, already faltering, tried,

"The witness mentioned something about . . ."

Paused,

"A pup being part of the struggle. What is this pup's name?"

Em, highly amused, dropped the remainder of the cig in the empty toddy glass, handed the glass to Costello, said,

"Be a dear, sweetie . . ."

Then, back to Ridge.

"Not sure you were entirely paying attention earlier, sergeant, but I did mention my recent sojourn in Korea."

Ridge looked fit to explode, snapped,

"Is there a point to this little . . . detour?"

Em gave her most beatific smile, said,

"Alas, I did, to my shame, pick up on one of their culinary customs . . ."

She stroked the pup's ears.

"I never name something I may later eat."

Quote from the *Sunday Times*:

Samantha Ellis believes that heroines such as
Scarlett O'Hara and Sylvia Plath's
Esther Greenwood are appealing precisely
because they behave so badly.
"I'd had so many good girl heroines," writes Ellis.
"Plath gave me a heroine who was anything but . . .
As Esther gets suicidal, she also gets *mean*.
She releases her inner bad girl, she picks up sailors,
reads scandal sheets, howls at her father's grave."

After Ridge left, I let out a long breath, said,

"Em, you know she will check the airlines."

Em pulled out her iPhone, five minutes of elegant, furious texting, and she smiled, said,

" 'Tis done and best if t'were done well."

I asked,

"Seriously, who the fuck are you?"

She was nuzzling her face against the pup's ears, said,

"The girl who just saved your ass from arrest. A thank-you about now might be good so feel free to jump in . . ."

Instead, I made her a kick-heart coffee, even lit her cig, asked,

"Were you in Arizona?"

She savored the coffee, said,

"I'd like it a bit more Sara Gran, you know, New Orleans, hint of chicory . . . yes, I went to rehab there."

Jesus wept!

"For which of your many personalities?"

"Jack, I have a near genius for math, tech stuff, but they say I'm a high-functioning sociopath."

She laughed, no humor touching her eyes, added,

"As in *Cowboy Junkies*, I am your skewed Misguided Angel and I need you to help to off the monster that is de Burgo."

"You have always managed to evade, like so much else, your motive, your hard-on for him."

Her phone buzzed . . . she read a text, put the pup gently aside, gathered her things, said,

"I'm Gone Girl."

Pecked me on the cheek, said,

"Catch you up for dinner, my treat tomorrow evening, and, oh . . . de Burgo . . .

he's my dad."

Using Google Search

Friends Reunite Ireland

I found Em's mother. She was living in a cottage in Kinvara. She was a "home-keeper," whatever the fuck that is. She was now using her maiden name, Marion McKee. Google Maps even showed me the cottage. The old adage:

"You want to know what the daughter
will become, meet the mother."

Worth a shot.

I went to Charley Byrne's Bookshop and wished Vinny a happy new year. He smiled ruefully at that. Then,

"So, what do you want, Jack?"

I did mock-offended.

"You think that's the only reason I'm here?"

"Pretty much."

I took a breath, asked,

"Could I borrow the van for a few hours?"

"You going into the book business, Jack?"

"Well, research of a sort."

He rooted around, then handed me the keys, said,

"Second gear needs a bit of cajoling."

Smiled at that, said,

"I will of course pay for the petrol."

"Yeah, like that will happen."

Em had only ever once referred to her mother, a throwaway quip:

"Good old Moms is a rummy."

The last time I read that description was in the early works of Hemingway. This in mind, I made a pit stop at an off-license, bought a bottle of brandy. The owner, handing me the bottle, asked,

"You want to buy a bundle of books?"

"Excuse me?"

He nodded at the van, which had a sign on the side:
CHARLEY BYRNE'S
NEW AND SECONDHAND BOOKS

I said,

"Not really."

He seemed surprised, pushed,

"Some James Pattersons in the bunch."

Jesus, how could I resist?

I found Marion McKee's cottage easily. Just look for the closed curtains. Alkies don't do light. I had a briefcase and my Garda coat, and looked like someone collecting the Household Tax. That is, like an asshole.

Took some banging on the door until she finally answered. A small woman in what used to be termed a housecoat,

or

camouflage.

Badly permed blond hair was sorely in need of help. Her eyes were tired, a little bloodshot, and her face, despite makeup, showed the savagery of alcohol. A stale reek of alcohol, nicotine, and fear emanated from her pores. I said,

"I need a few minutes of your time, about your daughter."

Saw the alarm, rushed,

"Nothing bad . . . quite good in fact. If I may?"

Indicating,

Let me in?

She did, reluctantly. The living room was small but obsessively tidy. Your life's going to shit, you try to hold something in place. She pointed to a chair that was forlorn in its loneliness. She sat on the couch, asked,

"May I offer you something, Mr . . . ?"

"Jack. No, I'm fine."

I put the briefcase on the table, pulled out a stack of papers, the bottle of brandy seemed to slip out. I smiled, said,

"Whoops, Christmas leftover."

And placed it on the table. Then, as if struck by a thought, said,

"How about we baptize this bad boy, to mark the good news about Em . . . or do you prefer Emerald?"

Her eyes locked on the bottle.

A beacon.

She fetched two glasses, heavy Galway crystal tumblers. I poured a passable amount into both, said,

"Here's to your daughter."

A fleeting dance across her eyes, fear chasing anxiety. She drained the brandy like a brawler. I stood up, glanced at her bookshelf, asked,

"May I . . . peruse? A compulsion of the trade."

Giving her the window. And, like a pro, fast, she replenished her glass and, I loved it, took a swig of mine. Oh, she was mighty, almost noble in her ruin. The books were like a legion of female artillery:

Germaine Greer

Naomi Wolf

Betty Friedan

And like a lost black sheep among the strident women, that out-of-favor, poor quasi-hippie, Richard Brautigan's

and peeking optimistically from a corner, Elizabeth Smart's

By Grand Central Station I Sat Down and Wept

Indeed.

I said,

"We are expanding the shop and wish to appoint Em as manager."

Marion tried to rouse some enthusiasm but blurted,

"She had been such a promising child."

I spied a pack of cigarettes, lit one, and, as I handed it to her, topped up her glass. She was rolling on a short recovery high, continued,

"But her father . . ."

deep brandied sigh,

"He claimed Emmy's dog had bitten him and she found . . ." mega gulp of brandy,

"The dog nailed to the shed door. He claimed some passing lunatic did it."

I was smart enough to stay quiet. I knew the stages of rapid morning drinking, and brandy? Well, fuck, it adds an extra dimension of apparent energy to a false alertness. She didn't as much smoke the cigarette as absorb it, her cheeks sucked to the bone as if the nicotine would grant absolution. Cresting now, reaching the anger stage,

"And the affairs, parading floozies in front of us, the renowned literary professor."

She looked at me as if I'd just appeared, dismissed me, said,

"I had money, you know, oh, yes but he . . . had something better, a shyster lawyer."

I looked at the bottle. Christ, how much had she drunk?

She hit a brief cloud of severe clarity, said,

"When she was seventeen, she went to him, after years of no contact. You know what he did? He hit on her! Isn't that the term nowadays and, when he realized who she was, he laughed and said, 'Roll your own.'"

I got out of there. Had put a blanket over her as she lay on the couch, called an ambulance. Driving away, I felt as low and dirty as any of the scumbags I'd ever laid a hurly on.

When I returned the van to Vinny, I said,

"I might be able to get you a deal on a batch of James Pattersons."

Got the look.

He said,

"Perfect! I'll add them to the five hundred copies of John Grisham adorning most of the Crime Section."

I was about to go, said,

"Hey, I believe you were on TV . . . that series, *Cities*?"

A rueful smile, then,

"It's all showbiz, Jack."

As he refused petrol money, I bought a shitload of books.

Jason Starr
Gerald Brenan
Eoin Colfer
Adrian McKinty
James Straley
Stanley Trybulski.

Asked,

"Any chance, Vinny, you can deliver them?"

He tipped his Facebook hat, said,

"Why we have the van."

Outside, I ran into Father Malachy, shrouded in cigarette smoke. I said,

"According to the papers, half the country's smokers have changed to e-cigarettes — vapors, as they're known."

He glanced at me, said,

"I'd rather be electrocuted."

"Be careful what you wish for, Father."

Dinner with Em.

She'd booked a table at Cooke's. The family who not only run a superior bookshop but probably the best restaurant in the city and bonus . . .

Pure Galway.

Billy Idol —

"White Wedding"

Yeah!

I had a Jameson. For the record, here's what Em ordered . . .

She opened with,

"Will you marry me?"

Never knowing when/if ever she was

(a) Herself/selves?

(b) Taking the piss.

I said,

"You're not pretty enough."

And fuck . . . her face fell, before I could say, "Hey
. . . kidding."

She ordered a large vodka tonic and I began my
Jameson march. After we got some of that knocked
down, we both pulled back a way, physically and
emotionally. She asked,

"Tell me what you're thinking."

I know, I know, you'll run with,

"You . . . dear."

The Jameson said,

"How it would be nice if just one person would fess
up to *12 Years a Slave* as eleven years too long."

She frowned, said,

"It's a masterpiece."

I sighed, tried,

"If I want torture porn, there's the *Saw* franchise.

Her starter arrived, she asked,

"Wanna share?"

"Like . . . our lives?"

By the time she reached dessert, she asked,

"Did you ever, like once, feel real love?"

"I feel it right now."

            Had to rush,

"for that little waif, Ziggy."

Then the image of Em's puppy nailed to the shed
door arose and I said,

"You should go visit your mother."

A mischievous dance in her eyes, she asked,

"And you, Jack, . . . care much for yours?"

Truth.

"She was a walking bitch, awash with piety, cunning in her constant cruelty . . . if there's a hell, I pray she roasts in it."

Em did a mock wipe of her brow, said,

"Phew, don't feel you have to hold back."

She reached across the table, touched my hand. I didn't recoil or flinch so some progress. She said,

"Jack, I am truly sorry for your young friend Boru. I really believed we could have saved him."

I had no answer.

Her hand still resting on mine, she held my gaze firmly, asked,

"I need a solemn pledge from you, Jack."

Fuck, it wouldn't be good. I tried deflection.

"Didn't we do the marriage gig at the start of the meal?"

Slapped my hand, stressed,

"Be serious, Jack."

"I'll give it a shot, what is it?"

"Next Friday, you have a table booked for two at Brannigan's. Be on time and don't leave until eleven o'clock. Make yourself . . . felt."

WTF?

"Sounds like I'm setting up an alibi."

Her hand withdrew. She said,

"Once, just once, don't be a stubborn bollix. Just humor me."

"What the hell, OK. Who am I dining with?"

Now got the pixie smile, made her look twelve, vulnerable, and, oh shit, I don't know . . . deeply exposed. She said,

"Part of an extended birthday buzz. You really need not to overthink this."

I nearly smiled, clichéd,

"Go with the flow."

She signaled for the check, snapped,

"Don't be a fuckhead. Just blew your shot at getting laid."

Through Boru's actual solicitor, I obtained his parents' address, bought a Mass card, had it signed by a priest in the Augustinians who was a human being, said,

"I am sorry for your loss."

More like him and the Church might have less to fear from lynch mobs. He was that rare to rarest man, one who by pure simplicity made you glad to be alive. Plus, it didn't cost an arm and a leg (limping or otherwise). I enclosed the following note:

Dear Mr. and Mrs. Kennedy,

No words can convey the loss you have endured. Forgive my enclosure of a Mass card but here, it's our sole feeble attempt to demonstrate our care.

Your son was a true gentleman, shining with intelligence, warmth, and utter charm. I was graced, honored, and humbled to be his friend. Know that, despite his brief time in our city, he became a true Galwegian. He will always live here in our hearts and we walk with deep respect the streets he grew to love.

He is a credit to you and a terrible loss to the very meaning of "life extraordinary."

With deepest sorrow,
Jack Taylor

If you want to know about spirituality, look into the eyes of a dog. So said William James. Ziggy was growing apace, already quirks of personality asserting themselves. He liked to nap on my Garda coat. Some long-lost tenuous connection to protection. He had brown velvet eyes that seemed to weep with emotion.

> *Acquiring a dog may be the only*
> *opportunity a human ever has to*
> *choose a relative.*

Cheeky little bugger too.

Already knew my favorite part of the couch for TV so he'd get there first. Like Glenn Close in *Fatal Attraction*, he seemed to have adopted the mantra

"I will not be ignored."

Times, too, he seemed to withdraw, his tiny body curling in on itself, emitting a deep sigh and ignoring all treats.

I'd done that gig my ownself.

I was currently watching the boxed set of

Van Veeteren

Maria Wern.

The latter was like Saga Nordén from *The Bridge*, without the icy autism.

Maria was a shade too fuckin whitebread.

Nordic noir rules.

I told Ziggy. He seemed unimpressed. Had the makings of a canine critic.

I wondered who Em had set me up to meet at Brannigan's. I'd given my word, so show up I would. Crossed my mind it might be de Burgo. Now that would make an interesting evening. Friday rolled around with the winds finally easing. The latest scandal was the Irish Water Board. Millions paid to a bunch of carpetbaggers to plan the installation of water meters in every home. First we endured years of poisoned water, now they'd charge us by the drop. The minister in charge of this fiasco, Phil Hogan, told us with his smug expression . . .

"*You can't make an omelet without . . .*"

I mean, he actually fuckin said that!

Brannigan's was off Kirwan's Lane. Had a reputation for great steaks. Ziggy whimpered as I prepared to leave. I told him,

"You guard the apartment . . . you know, do dog stuff."

He ignored me.

I walked down Shop Street, trying to adjust the tie I'd worn. Under my Garda coat I had my sports jacket and, from a distance, might even have passed for respectable. Just past Easons, a man stepped out of the lane. Young, in an expensive Burberry coat, so it wasn't until he spoke that I realized who he was. The gap where his previous magnificent teeth had been. The punk who'd been beating on Ziggy. He snarled,

"You think you got away with it, Taylor?"

He kept a distance, so he had learned something from our encounter.

I asked,

"You want something?"

Bravado and caution fought in his face. He said,

"You stole my wallet."

I smiled, said,

"Put it down to a fine for disorderly conduct."

His hands were in his pockets and a debate was raging in his mind. He settled for,

"You'll pay for it, Taylor."

I shook my head, said.

"Hey, I'm here now, why wait?"

He turned, scuttled back into the lane. I said,

"That's what I thought."

I was standing in the reception area of Brannigan's. A pleasing aroma of charcoal/grill/barbecue gave me that rare but fleeting feeling,

An appetite!

Throw in a hint of anxiety/anticipation and you're, if not raring to go, certainly on the precipice.

I saw Ridge approach, a puzzled expression in place. She was dressed for an evening out. An almost too-tight little black number, semi-killer heels, highlights in her hair, caution in her eyes. We almost said in unison,

. . . What are you doing here?

I checked with the maître d'. Hard to even write that with an Irish accent. The reservation for two was in the

216

name of Semple (or if you wanted to push buttons, Simple.)

Ridge got there first.

"Someone thinks we should meet?"

I rolled, said,

"Maybe to help us rekindle a friendship."

Raised her eyes, said,

"Take more than a bloody dinner."

I wanted to slap her, pleaded,

"For just one fucking time . . . chill."

A waitress approached, asked,

"Would Mr. and Mrs. Semple care for a complimentary cocktail before dinner?"

Ridge nearly relented.

I said,

"One drink?"

She agreed.

The barman was one of those people whom Kevin Bridges described as

"Never having been punched in the face."

His enthusiasm to see us was grating. He beamed,

"And what can I tempt you fine folk with this evening?"

Mario Rosenstock would have loved him! All that plastic blarney. Ridge snarled,

"Assault and battery."

I interceded, said,

"Two frozen margaritas."

Add more ice to the chill Ridge trailed. I made a T gesture to the guy, indicating

"Large amount of tequila or trouble."

I think he'd already caught the gist of the latter. I said,

"Ridge, you look nice."

Didn't fly.

She said,

"I thought my ex-husband was surprising me."

The drinks came, I raised my glass, said,

"Slainte."

"Whatever."

She took a lethal taste, color rising to her cheeks. I realized she might have had a preparatory one . . . or two.

I tried,

"Perhaps dinner would go some way to us reconnecting?"

She ignored that, asked,

"Where's the psycho bitch?"

I gave her a tequila smile, said,

"Good title for a self-help book."

She studied me for a long minute, gave a mock sigh, said,

"You can't rile me anymore."

She was oh, so wrong about that. It was simply that goading ran so close to deep hurt that I backed off, asked,

"No way back to our former friendship then?"

The barman approached with a fresh pitcher, asked,

"You folks like to go for broke?"

I nodded.

Tequila is a sly son of a bitch. Tastes so good, you truly believe . . . briefly . . . it won't kick. I coasted on that lie, rode the fake euphoria, risked,

218

"I miss you."

She was lost in some other thought, then snapped back, said,

"We were scattered with the ashes of Stewart."

Fuck!

I spat,

"Damn near poetry."

She gathered her things, threw some notes onto the bar, tip for the barman, said,

"No, Jack, poetry was Stewart with his insane belief in you. What we've got is ashes in the mouth."

And she was gone.

The barman took her empty glass, dared,

"Tough cookie."

I finished my drink, said,

"If you only knew the half of it."

Checked my watch, we'd managed all of forty-five minutes, not a moment of it civil.

My mobile rang at two o'clock in the morning. The pup, sound asleep on my chest, simply moved to the warm part of the bed. I growled,

"What the fuck —"

"Jack, it's Em."

"Christ, this is a surprise. Don't you sleep?"

Her voice had urgency.

"How did the evening go?"

I nearly smiled but stayed in hard-ass mode, asked,

"You seriously thought you could get us to reconcile?"

More urgent.

"What time did ye stay until?"

"Hmmm . . . she stayed, I think, almost forty-five minutes."

Rage.

"What? You left within an hour? You stupid bastard, couldn't you do one bloody thing right?"

"Hey . . . hey . . . take a fuckin breath. She left, I didn't."

Hope.

"You stayed on?"

"Sure, even ordered steaks for two. Got them to do a doggy bag — reluctantly I might add. Ziggy will be having prime for the next few days."

Relief.

"And so you were noticed, right? I mean people remember you?"

My brain kicked in, I said,

"If I didn't know better I'd say you were giving me an alibi."

Dawning.

"Em . . . Jesus, is that it?"

Dead air.

The Irish Water Board, continuing to threaten, bully, and intimidate the population, refuses to release details of massive bonuses and perks. It does emerge that three hundred of its staff attended a "laughter yoga" workshop in Croke Park in 2013. The theory is you guffaw for fifteen minutes and this is good for body and mind.

The people haven't had much to laugh at for many years. A workshop seems out of their reach.

The Guards came early. A heavy pounding at the door.
The pup trailed at my heels as I went down to open
it. Two in uniform. Number one was vaguely familiar to
me as a hurler. Number two was of the new gung-ho
variety. Number one gave me a nod, not unfriendly,
said,

"Jack, they want to talk to you at the station."

They followed me in as I threw on some clothes. The
pup took an instant dislike to number two, yapping and
nipping at his ankles. The guy said,

"Control that animal or I'll give him a kicking."

I snatched Ziggy up, put him in the bedroom with
some treats, closed the door, said,

"Trust me, it would be the last kicking you'd give."

He looked at number one, then blushed,

"Is that a threat, sir?"

Number one said,

"Ah, shut up."

We drove to the station in silence. I let my mind go
into the zero zone, focusing on nothing. I'd been this
route many times.

I was brought into Superintendant Clancy's office. In
full regalia, he was behind his massive desk. A scowl in
place. Sitting to his left was Ridge, no smile of welcome.
The two Guards stood behind me. Clancy adopted a
fake warmth.

"Ah Jack, good of you to come."

I said,

"I'd a choice?"

Clancy flipped through some papers, then,

"Professor de Burgo was found murdered on Friday evening. Can you account for your whereabouts between eight and eleven that evening?"

My mind tried to grasp the implications but, before I could answer, Ridge leaped to her feet, shouted,

"He has a bloody alibi . . . it's me. I was with him."

And she stormed out of the office. A silence followed, then Clancy paced.

"Lovers' tiff?"

I asked,

"How was he killed?"

A beat before,

"A nail through his forehead."

Then waved his hand, dismissing me. I said,

"You can cross another suspect off your list."

His head moved, slight interest.

"And who might that be?"

"Boru Kennedy."

He shook his head,

"Not known to me, I'm afraid."

I turned to go, said,

"Of course not. Why would you remember a young man who hanged himself in prison on Christmas eve? He had been cleared of putting a nail through his girlfriend's head."

Em vanished. As if she'd never been. No e-mails, texts, nothing. I missed her. But the pup filled the void. I bought him a small Galway United scarf and he seemed delighted with its fit.

I took him, or rather he took me, for daily walks and I became reacquainted with my city. Feeding the swans was, of course, on our agenda. Oddly, after a few visits, the swans tolerated him. He could move along the shore and the slipway without them hissing. I kept a wary eye. Best not to fuck with these beautiful creatures.

He didn't.

The evenings were getting a stretch to them and I'd see Ziggy, outlined against the bay, his scarf blowing gently, the swans dotted around him. He'd stand on the pier watching them glide. I could see his sharp mind thinking,

"Shit, I could do that."

One evening, on our way back, standing on a wall by the Claddagh was the thug whose teeth I had removed. He was staring, dead-eyed, not at me but at the pup. Then he turned to me, made the cutthroat motion slowly across his neck with his right hand

223

. . . and smiled.

The teeth had been replaced. I shouted,

"Now all you need to get is a set of balls."

But he was gone.

As spring slowly began to creep up, we got back to the flat and in the middle of the kitchen was . . .

A tiny green emerald.

Manchester United continued their losing streak as they made a record-breaking bid to buy Chelsea's Spanish, Le Meta. I said to Ziggy,

"The Six Nations Cup will begin soon."

He seemed more rapt in Paul O'Grady's series on the Battersea Dogs Home. The pup disliked cigarette smoke so I took the odd cig outside. Too much drink and he sensed my loss of control, responded by whimpering. I cut way back. He was whipping me into shape.

Tuesday morning, St. Anthony's Day, I was sitting on a bench in Claddagh. Ziggy was down on the shore, his sense of smell in overdrive from all the different stimuli. A well-dressed woman approached and sat on the bench. Her handbag? I saw an article in the *Galway Advertiser* quoting some lunatic price for these suckers. Plus a six-month waiting period to purchase! Jesus, you could order a Harley in less time. She obviously had not been among those who had to wait.

She smiled, said,

"That your little dog on the shore?"

I nodded.

She said,

"He keeps checking you're still here."

I gave a noncommittal smile.

Then she put out her hand, said,

"I'm Alison Reid. I already know you're Jack Taylor."

I took her hand, noting the thin gold Rolex, said,

"Nice to meet you."

And waited.

She cleared her throat, said,

"My husband died a long time ago and all I really have is one brother."

I wanted to say,

"Fascinating, but should I give a fuck why?"

Went with,

"My condolences."

No maneuver room there. But she tried,

"My brother was killed recently and the Guards appear to have abandoned the case. A Superintendent Clancy suggested you might help. Said you were a form of a forlorn St. Jude. For hopeless cases?"

Clancy fucking with me. I whistled for Ziggy, stood, said,

"I'm very sorry but I'm temporarily out of the business."

I was putting the lead on Ziggy, she handed me a card, said,

"If you might reconsider, I would reward your time generously."

I shoved the card into my jeans, said,

"Nice talking to you."

We'd gotten about five yards when she called,

"That's my business card, it's my maiden name.

I didn't snap . . .

Whatever!

That evening as Ziggy and I shared a pot of Irish stew with a hint of Jameson, the card slipped out of my pocket. Picked it up, read:

Alison de Burgo.

The sound, the feel of some words linger in my mouth. There is almost a joy in uttering the Danish TV series,

Forbrydelsen,

a current favorite. The translation now seems bitterly apt on that wet, stormy Saturday. I had the lead ready for Ziggy but the sound of the storm discouraged him. Maybe he had flashbacks to the evening I found him. So I said,

"It's OK, buddy. You snuggle up on the couch, I'll get the shopping and be back in jig time." Earlier, when I'd been playing with him, the joy in his little body so overwhelmed him that he lay back, gave a yawn/sigh to release it. I tickled his ears, then headed out.

The wind was fierce, with a cold rain lashing across the streets. I'd gotten the shopping and stopped for brief shelter near Garavan's. A ne'er-do-well named Jackson coerced me into a fast pint.

I did delay a bit. The chat was lively and the pub was warm, whispering:

"Stay a little longer."

Guilt-ridden, I pushed out of there, way past my intended plan. Struggled against the wind, got my keys out, juggling the groceries. My front door was wide open. A hard kick had taken it completely off the hinges. My heart lurched.

The pup literally had been torn apart. His tiny head was left on the arm of the couch. A sheet of paper underneath, awash in blood, but clearly scrawled on it was:

"Doggone."

Em had said to me one time,

"Yo, Dude (*sic*), if I'm not, like, around, and you need me, e-mail me at

Greenhell@gmail.com.

Sick and near broken, I did e-mail her and outlined the events of the last few days and ended with

"Sometimes there's just no justice. The bad guys do live, if not happily ever after, then certainly conspicuously."

She didn't reply.

At least not by e-mail.

You might say her reply was more biblical, and definitely more colorful.

At the tennis championships in Melbourne, one of the players had a tattoo in Celtic print. From Beckett, it read:

I can't go on, I won't go on . . . I'll go on.

A month later, almost to the day, the head of a young man was found, wrapped in a blanket, outside Galway City's dog shelter.

Newspapers variously described the blanket as dark blue and dull green, but one tabloid, in a fanciful piece, described it as "emerald green."

Identifying the young man was proving difficult as his teeth had been removed.

Returning to the flat on a fine Sunday evening, I found a small Labrador pup in a box at my door. I cried,

"I can't . . . Jesus, I just can't!"

Can I?

I bent down to touch the warm little head. He was sleeping soundly on my Garda coat. Then I noticed he was wearing a shiny new leather collar.

Green.

A medallion attached had his name. I had to squint to read it.

BORU.